Humans are the worst monsters

Shadows of
Samantha

Derek Wachter

twelve

Table of Contents

"Human trafficking is a multi-billion dollar growth industry because, unlike drugs, which are gone as soon as they are used, humans can be recycled. Because they can continue to be exploited, they're a better investment for traffickers."

- Terry Coonan

Chapter 1: Chicago, Illinois

A school bell rang in the 6th grade classroom for the last time in the school year at Park Forest Middle School. The last day of school came to a close at exactly 2:35 PM on a Wednesday afternoon in Park Forest, a small suburban village south of Chicago, Illinois. Elizabeth Owen waited in her car in the student pickup area for her daughter Samantha to walk out the main doors of the school and out onto the sidewalk. It didn't take long before the front doors of the school were propped open by a couple of teachers wearing bright orange and yellow neon safety vests as students filtered out of the front of the building. Among the sea of children was Elizabeth's daughter, Samantha.

A young girl, twelve years old, yet mature and intelligent beyond her years. She walked out of the school, wearing blue jeans and a pink shirt with Crystal Mountain cartoon characters on it—her favorite cartoon show on the television. Her dark brown hair hung down past her shoulders to about the midpoint of her back, draped over her green backpack. The young girl paused for a moment as children moved to and from around her. As she oriented herself, she looked out and saw her mom's large Suburban parked near the front of the school. Her mother walked around the back of It towards her and up onto the sidewalk. When she saw Elizabeth approaching, Samantha took off running, darting through the crowd of students until she reached her mom and gave her a hug on the sidewalk.

"Hi honey, how was your last day of sixth grade?" asked Elizabeth.

"It was good. I picked up my yearbook on the way out, and they used the picture of Amanda, Taylor, and I when we were at the bowling alley on New Year's Eve. It's on page eighteen, Mom, look!" said Samantha as she thumbed through the pages from the beginning to the middle of the small photo book.

"That's great, honey, come walk to the car with me and show me in there. We need to head home. Your dad has a surprise for us when he gets off work here in the next couple hours."

"A surprise?"

"Yes, he wants to talk to us about summer vacation this year. He has something big planned."

"Are we going to that water park in Iowa again? Can I invite my friends?"

"If we are going to that water park in Iowa, then yes, we can invite your friends, honey."

"Cool!"

"What else did you do today?" asked her mom as the two walked up to the Suburban, Elizabeth opening the passenger door for her daughter as she climbed up and in.

"We watched a movie in Mr. Jenning's class today."

Elizabeth shut the passenger door and walked around the front of the Suburban as Samantha buckled herself in, nestling her backpack on the floor between her feet, leaving her sixth-grade yearbook on the dashboard. Elizabeth opened the driver's side door, got in and started the Suburban.

"You watched a movie in Mr. Jenning's class today?" She asked her daughter as she buckled herself into the driver's seat.

"Ya, we did!" replied Samantha with excitement in her voice.

"Which movie did you watch?"

Elizabeth started the car, put it in gear, and drove out of the school parking lot as she turned onto the road.

"Charlie and the Chocolate Factory."

"Oh my. I remember watching that when I was in the third grade, too. It was the first time I had ever seen that movie in my life. How did you like it?"

"I liked the ending when the elevator went up high into the sky."

"Oh yes, that was a pretty special moment in the movie," said Elizabeth, laughing.

"How was your day, Mom?"

"Oh, it was good. I worked half a day today and left the campus at 12:30. Went to the dentist and got my teeth cleaned at 1:00, and then just got out twenty minutes ago and came to pick you up."

"Have you heard from Dad?"

"We chatted for a little bit before I left the college today. That's when he told me he wanted to talk with us this evening at dinner about summer vacation this year."

"What's for dinner tonight?"

"I have the soup that you like in the crock-pot simmering as we speak."

"That chicken soup thing you wanted to experiment with?"

"That's right."

"With grilled cheese sandwiches?"

"Yup."

"Are you putting the celery and carrots in the soup this time?"

"I sure will be."

"Good! I like carrots and celery in the soup."

"So does your dad too. Honey, I need to stop at the store and run in to grab some pepper. We're out of pepper at the house, and your dad likes pepper with his soup."

"Okay, Mom."

"Do you want to come in with me?"

"No, I'll stay in the car and look through my yearbook."

"Sounds good. That's a big book this year," said Elizabeth.

"It's almost eighty full pages of color photos."

"Fun. You guys have your school pictures in there too?"

"Ya, they're at the end of the book."

Elizabeth pulled into the parking lot of the town's grocery store. A Piggly Wiggly store with a large stock of groceries, produce, and frozen foods. Finding a parking spot near the front of the store, Elizabeth parked the car in a stall. She turned the ignition off and stuffed the keys into her purse as she slung the purse strap over her shoulder.

"Okay, I won't be too long. Just running in to grab some pepper."

"What about ice cream?"

"I got a carton of chocolate a couple of days ago."

"Okay, that works."

"Okay, honey." Elizabeth laughed. "I'll be right back."

She got out and shut the door as Samantha locked the doors behind her. She thumbed through the pages of her yearbook, finding pictures of her friends and the other kids at the school, even finding pictures of herself and all the good times that she had over the past school year. It was hard to believe that in just a couple of years she would be a freshman in high school. Time was moving fast in her life for sure, as the seventh grade wasn't too far away now. Samantha thumbed towards the center of the book and found another picture of her and four of her friends on a school field trip to the River Cruise of Architecture in Chicago. It was a big field trip at the beginning of the school year back in September. She loved every minute of that trip. Being on a boat was a wonderful experience and something that she would like to experience again someday.

As she thumbed forward in the yearbook, Samantha heard the door belonging to the car next to her open. She glanced up and saw a man in his mid-40s through the passenger-side window. A scar ran up the left side of his face from the jawbone up to his eye. He wore a black goatee, along with short black hair, and brown walnut-colored eyes. The man stared at Samantha as she sat in the front seat of the car, never taking his eyes off her. He looked like a statue instead of an actual human being. He startled Samantha, making her feel anxious as she thought he had malicious intentions on his mind.

Samantha stared into his eyes when the driver's side car door opened, startling Samantha and causing her to jump in her seat and turn around, only to see it was her mom getting back into the driver's seat.

"Hey, scaredy cat. What's wrong with you?"

Samantha turned back around and looked out the passenger side window, but no one was there. She looked in the passenger-side mirror and saw the man walking away towards the store, with his back turned to her.

"Nothing. I'm fine, Mom."

"Okay. I grabbed some gummy bears for you while I was in there, too. I know you like them," she said, handing them to Samantha.

"Thank you, Mom." She took the small bag of colorful gummy bears and set it down on the center console of the Suburban.

"You need anything before we go home?" her mom asked as she secured the seat belt across her waist.

"No, I'm fine, Mom."

Starting the truck, Elizabeth took off and out of the parking lot. She pulled out onto the street and started their drive home.

Park Forest is a small town located just south of the bigger city of Chicago. The town was originally designated years ago to be a community for veterans returning from the Second World War back to America. Elizabeth and her husband Anthony moved to the area back in 2008 as a newlywed couple, when Anthony got his employment with Hackenberry and Sanderlin—one of the local law firms based on the south side of Chicago. Soon after moving to the area, Elizabeth finished her master's program and became a teacher at the local high school near Park Forest. She taught English literature for a few years before she taught at South Side Community College and worked full time as a professor of English. After both Elizabeth and Anthony were set in their respective careers for a few years, they had Samantha. Born on Christmas Eve in 2012, she was the best Christmas gift that the young couple could have asked for. Having Samantha didn't slow them down, though. Like any other couple, they effectively balanced the roles of being parents and full-time workers.

The street the family lived on was in a decent middle-class neighborhood. Brown Lake Road was a typical neighborhood in the Park Forest area. Kids trick-or-treat on Halloween night, and houses hang up lights and decorations for Christmas. Even old Parker Cunnigham in the house at the end of the block would dress up as the Easter bunny every year and be out in the early morning hours, hiding eggs around the neighborhood for the kids. For living in the suburbs of Chicago, this wasn't a bad little place to be.

Elizabeth turned her truck onto Brown Lake Road and drove halfway down the street, when she turned into her driveway and opened the garage door of a beautiful tan colored two level home. Each house featured a well-manicured front lawn. Children's bicycles lay on the ground in the driveways or on the grass, too. She parked the Suburban inside the garage and stopped the vehicle.

Samantha opened the door on her side of the truck, jumped out and shut it while Elizabeth was getting out herself. With her yearbook in one hand and backpack in the other, she walked up to the door that led into the house and opened it. Reaching up, she pushed the button on the wall next to the door and closed the garage door while her mom followed behind her.

"Dinner will be in a couple of hours, Sam. Put your stuff away and then store your backpack in the hallway closet, okay?"

"Okay, Mom."

"Can you help me cut up some carrots and celery here in a little bit?"

"Sure, Mom, I can," said Samantha as she went upstairs to her bedroom on the second floor.

She went into her bedroom, putting her backpack down on the bed. She walked over to the small desk by the window and set her yearbook down on the desk. She turned and walked back to her bed, opening her pack up and taking two books and a binder out. As she put her school supplies away, she looked out the window and saw her dad pulling into the driveway. She smiled as she picked up the binder and book and stuffed them onto the shelves that still had a little room left over from the books and magazines that were already there. After cramming the last book onto the shelf, she heard the door open from the garage into the kitchen and heard her dad's voice.

"Hey Liz, how was your day?" said her father, shortly followed by the sound of a kiss.

"It was good. Held a lecture for a couple of classes this morning, had a couple of student meetings later in the morning and then left midway through the day to go to my appointment and pick up Sam."

"How was her last day of school?"

"Good. She got a yearbook from her class today. She's upstairs unpacking her bag."

Samantha finished unpacking her backpack, taking the last bits of used paper and gum wrappers out and tossing them into the wastebasket. She turned and left her room, heading downstairs to meet her parents in the kitchen. She walked into the kitchen; she saw her dad and mom hugging there by the kitchen sink.

"Hi Daddy," she said with a smile on her face and her backpack in hand.

"Hi honey, how are you doing?" asked Anthony as he let go of his wife and walked over, giving his only daughter a hug.

"Fine," she said, hugging him back. "We just got home, and I'm coming down to help Mom cut up some vegetables."

"Well, be careful cutting," said Anthony.

"It's fine, Dad. I'm using the vegetable cutter machine," replied Samantha.

"Speaking of that, what is for dinner tonight?"

"Going to make that chicken soup I tried last month," said Elizabeth.

"Are you putting the carrots and celery into the soup this time?"

"Yes, that's what Sam is going to dice up for me. Along with the green beans and red potatoes too."

"Sounds good. Do we have any black pepper?"

"I stopped on the way home and got some."

"Thanks, dear. I'm going to the bedroom for a minute, but I'll be right back to help set the table. I got some news to share with you guys tonight about our family trip this summer."

"Sounds good. We'll be right here."

Anthony went up the stairs to their bedroom while Samantha and her mom stayed in the kitchen and prepped dinner. Elizabeth washed the vegetables and cut them in half while Samantha used the vegetable chopper to chop the vegetables into smaller pieces. A short time later, Anthony came back from the bedroom dressed in lounging clothes for the evening and helped set the table for dinner.

When Samantha finished chopping the vegetables, she stuffed them into the crockpot with the soup and chicken. Elizabeth dumped pre-cooked rice into the crockpot as well and covered the pot with the lid. Turning it to the hot setting, the family went out to the living room and watched television for a little bit. Samantha had gone back up to her room while her parents relaxed on the couch together. Samantha drew in her coloring book until she heard her mom calling her back downstairs to the dining room table. Dinner was ready.

She finished coloring a beachball in her coloring book, then put the crayons away and came downstairs just as her dad took his spot at the table and set down a pitcher of water. Samantha joined them at the table as her mom served the soup and took a seat.

"What were you working on in your room, kiddo?" asked her dad as he poured a glass of ice-cold water for himself.

"Just working in that coloring book that I got for my birthday a couple months back."

"You really enjoy that book, huh?"

"I do."

"Hey, you guys know what's for dessert tonight?"

"There's dessert?"

"Of course. Chocolate ice cream!" said her mom.

"Great!" yelled Samantha, excited by the thought of chocolate ice cream.

"But before all that, I have an announcement to make tonight, you guys," said Anthony.

"Each year we all take a family vacation. Last year we went to Yellowstone National Park. The year before that, we went on a cruise down to the Caribbean. This year, however, I was telling your mom, Sam." He paused, eating a spoonful of his soup. "This year I have managed to secure us some seats on a flight down to Florida to go to the Crystal Coast Kingdom in Miami!"

"What! No way!" said Samantha.

"Yes way!" replied her dad. "Now, your mom is teaching one summer school class this year. And that is an online Internet class through the college, too. Which means she won't have a hard time getting time off. Or she can find an instructor's aide to help for the week and run the class while she takes time off."

"I'll probably do that, honey. Just take the week off. The instructor's aide, Cindy, has always wanted a chance to run the class. This will be a good opportunity for her to take charge of things and see how she does for a week."

"Even better then. So that will be the plan. This year we're going to leave on Sunday, July third. Then we won't be back home until Tuesday, July eleventh. I spoke with our travel agent today, and she is securing us plane tickets down to Miami. We can get a taxi at the airport to take us to the hotel at the theme park. Angie is going to get us a reservation for a week at the resort."

"How much will that all cost us?" asked Elizabeth, eating a spoonful of soup.

"Well, here's the best part of it. If we stay at the resort in the park, then we get a discount. Angie is looking through these options for us too. Altogether, this trip will probably cost us closer to three thousand dollars. Which, for a full week, isn't too bad."

"What about meals?" asked Elizabeth.

"Yeah, what about meals?" Said Samantha, reiterating what her mom just said as she ate a spoonful of soup as well.

"Supplied by the resort. So, when you stay at the resort you get breakfast and dinner provided, and the only meal we would have to buy is lunch."

"Oh, so like how the cruise ship worked out then," said Elizabeth.

"Yeah, like how the cruise ship worked out," said Samantha.

"That's right, very similar to that," replied Anthony.

"Can I bring a friend with us?" Samantha asked.

"You can ask a friend if you'd like, sure," said Anthony. "So that's the big news. What do you think, Sam?"

"I can't wait!"

"Honey, do you want to also share with your dad about your yearbook you got today too?" asked Elizabeth.

The family sat together and had dinner, conversing with one another and enjoying their time together. They talked about Samantha's last day of school, Elizabeth's work, and what they were going to be doing for the weekend together.

After dinner, they helped clean up together, then sat down and enjoyed a Friday night movie night while Anthony and Elizabeth talked in more detail about the trip in July. Samantha went upstairs to her bedroom and got changed into her pajamas, then came back downstairs and sat on the couch between her parents. She made it partway through the movie before she fell asleep on the couch, laying her head down on her father's lap. That evening she had dreams of summer vacation. Spending time with friends. Enjoying the summer to come.

After the movie was over, her dad got up and helped pick her up as Elizabeth turned the TV off and shut the lights off. Taking her upstairs, her father laid her in bed while her mom shut the last of the lights off and went upstairs too. Anthony pulled the bed sheets back and laid her down. As he covered her up with the covers, Samantha stirred awake and saw her dad standing there by the bed.

"Goodnight, Daddy," she said as she rolled over onto her side, facing the wall.

"Goodnight, sweetheart. Sweet dreams," he said as he turned the nightlight on and left the room.

Meeting Elizabeth in the hallway, the two looked at their daughter for a moment as Anthony shut the door to her bedroom for the night.

"Won't get many more opportunities like that, Liz," said Anthony.

"I would say in a couple of years' time she'll be wanting to spend time with her friends, and less time with us," replied Elizabeth.

"You and I were like that."

"Oh, speak for yourself. I was always hanging out with my parents on Friday nights."

"Sure, until you met me in high school. Then you were hanging out with me all the time," said Anthony, as the couple walked to their bedroom.

"You think she was excited about the trip?" asked Elizabeth, walking into the bedroom and flipping the light switch on.

"I think so. She loved the Crystal Coast Kingdom pictures she saw on the internet before. The rides and park characters."

"Well, it will be a nice trip. It'll be nice staying at the park's resort hotel too."

"So much easier than leaving the park and traveling to a hotel miles away. We can just walk to our hotel there in the park. Plus, they have a pool, sauna, and water slides. Really, we could make a whole day out of just staying at the resort and the pool," said Anthony, pulling back the bedsheets on his side of the bed.

"Well, I'm looking forward to it. I think this will be a very memorable trip," said Elizabeth.

"I'm sure it will be, too," said Anthony as he went to the bathroom to brush his teeth and wash his face before going to bed.

Elizabeth joined him at the dual sink, and they both brushed their teeth. When they finished, they both put on their pajamas and crawled into bed together. Curling up next to one another, they fell asleep peacefully for the night, ready to take on the weekend ahead of them together.

Chapter 2: Chicago to O'Hare International Airport

"Honey, take your suitcase upstairs for me and set it on your bed. I'll be up in a minute to help you get it packed, okay?" said Elizabeth as she pulled Samantha's suitcase out from the top of a shelf along the side wall in the garage. She handed the suitcase down to Samantha, who did what she was told and took the case from her mom. She brought the light blue suitcase into the house and took it upstairs, putting it down on her bed. When she did, a spider quickly ran off the side of the suitcase and onto the bed. Samantha screeched, then quickly took a shoe from the floor. After smashing the bug on the bed and killing it, she cleaned up the dead spider with a tissue and discarded it in the garbage can in her room. Samantha then went back downstairs to the garage and helped her mom with the rest of the luggage.

"Here's your father's luggage, honey. Can you take that and set that down in the kitchen?" asked her mom, handing her another piece of luggage from the shelf.

"Sure mom. What time is Dad coming home today?" asked Samantha, taking the suitcase from her mom and setting it on the floor of the garage.

"Dad's getting off work early. So, he can come home and pack for the trip. Your dad always seems to wait until the last minute to pack his clothes for a trip."

Elizabeth pulled out her suitcase from the shelf, turned on the ladder and handed it to her too. Samantha took it from her mom and set it down next to her dad's luggage.

"Okay, I think that is it," said Elizabeth as she stepped down off the ladder.

"What are we doing for dinner tonight?" asked Samantha.

"Pizza. Making it simple so we don't have to do a bunch of dishes tonight and we can get to bed early to be at the airport.

"Can Emily come over and hang out for dinner?" asked Samantha.

"Of course she can. I'm sorry she couldn't come along with us on this trip. I know you were disappointed."

"It's okay, Mom. She'll have fun on her own trip with her parents too."

"Next year she can tag along with us. I guess her parents and we could have communicated better rather than planning our trips at the same time."

"It's okay, Mom."

"Is she leaving tomorrow, or on Monday?"

"She's leaving tomorrow too."

"And they're going to San Antonio this year to visit her grandparents?" asked Elizabeth, grabbing one of the suitcases and taking it with her as she walked back into the house.

"Yup," said Samantha as she took the second case and brought it in with her.

"Well, good for them. I hope they have safe travels. Did you want to call her on the phone?"

"Oh, I was just going to text her on my phone and let her know, Mom."

"Oh, of course. Let her know that I can take her home tonight, so she doesn't have to walk home in the dark too. Then afterwards we can get our cases packed and loaded in the car for the airport tomorrow."

"Where do you want me to put your suitcases, Mom?"

"Can you take them upstairs and put them in our room, honey?"

"Sure, Mom."

Samantha took the suitcase from her mom and walked it up the stairs to their bedroom. Sitting them up at the foot of the bed, she left their room and went into her room, grabbed her phone, and sent a message to her friend.

Hey Emily. We're having pizza tonight at my house. Do you want to come over for dinner? Mom said that she can bring you home tonight, so you don't have to walk home in the dark.

Samantha waited for a few minutes, laying down on her bed in the process. She set the phone down on her stomach, waiting until it vibrated, then checked it.

"Hey Sam! Thanks for the offer, but I can't tonight. Grandma is coming over this evening, and we have a big dinner planned."

"No problem. Are you guys still leaving Monday morning?"

"Yeah. Leaving early too. Dad was talking about leaving for the airport at 5am."

"Dang, that's early."

Emily responded back to her message quickly. *"What time are you guys leaving?"*

"We're flying out at 10:30 AM."

"We'll, you don't have to get up as early as I do."

"Right? You want to come over before dinner?"

"Would love to, but I can't. Mom wants me packed up today and all the luggage in the car so we can just eat dinner quick and get to bed early tonight so we can be at the airport tomorrow morning."

"Okay, Emily. You text me when you're on your trip, and I'll text you too."

"Okay, Sam. Love you."

"Love you too, have fun and safe travels."

"Thanks, you too."

Samantha turned the texting app off on her phone and switched over to a music app. Turning it on, she listened to her music as she fell asleep.

Waking up a short time later, she realized she had slept almost a whole hour. She turned her music off, and the room went silent until she heard two voices talking downstairs. She went back downstairs and saw her mom and dad resting on the couch, looking over a couple of brochures of the theme park they were visiting for the week. Anthony looked up and saw that his daughter had just made her way down the stairs.

"Hey honey. How are you?"

"Fine. I just took a nap."

"Did you invite Emily over for dinner tonight?" asked Elizabeth.

"I did, but she is having dinner tonight with her family. Her grandma is coming over for dinner."

"Well, that sounds nice for them," said Anthony.

"Hey, do you want to see all the different things to do at the theme park?" asked Elizabeth.

Samantha joined them on the couch, and her mom showed her the theme park's brochures displaying all the different rides available at the park. They also saw the various restaurants at the resort, and even activities nearby, outside of the park. She saw the different monorails and transportation available to get from one side of the park to the other, the different pools, and water rides. They talked about all the evening events, which included shows with the characters of the park, fireworks, parades, and much more. There was so much to see, do, and experience there in the park, Samantha was thinking about how they would be able to get it all done in just a week.

"Oh, jeez. I should probably think about ordering the pizza soon," said Anthony.

"Where did you want to order from, hon?" asked Elizabeth.

"I was thinking probably Figgaroa's on the north side of town."

"Are they the ones that have that deep dish that we liked so much?"

"Ya, they are. I was thinking about trying the Colorado deep dish this time. With ham, pepperoni, peppers, mushrooms, and olives."

"That sounds good. Honey, what are you wanting from there?" Elizabeth asked, turning to Samantha.

"Extra cheese, please."

"Simple enough. Honey, is that Colorado deep dish good or do you want something else?"

"No, that's fine with me, honey."

"Okay, I'll give them a call."

Anthony handed his brochure to Samantha as he stood up and walked into the kitchen to get the phone number off the Figgaroa's magnet that was on the refrigerator door.

"Well, I'm going to head upstairs to our bathroom and take a hot bath while you guys run up the road to get the pizza. Did you want to go with your dad? I'm sorry. I suppose I should have asked if you wanted to go or not."

"No, it's fine. I'll go with dad."

"Okay. Well, here is another magazine. Look through them and get an idea for some shows you want to see, rides you want to ride, and characters you want to meet and let us know, okay?"

"Okay, Mom."

Elziabeth got up from the couch and handed the magazine to her daughter before heading upstairs for a bath. Meanwhile, Samantha thumbed through the magazine with excitement. Anthony called and ordered pizza in the kitchen, and when he hung up the phone, he came back into the living room.

"Okay, honey. Pizza will be ready in about half an hour. Want to come with me to pick it up?"

"Yeah, I'll come with."

"Where's your mom?"

"She went upstairs to take a bath before dinner."

"Oh, okay. Go ahead and get in the car, honey. Here are the keys. Let yourself in. I'm going to let Mom know we're taking off."

"Okay, Dad," said Samantha as she set the magazine down on the couch.

She grabbed the keys from her dad. As he turned and went up the stairs to their bedroom, Samantha let herself out into the garage through the door in the kitchen. She opened the garage door and unlocked the car. After getting into the passenger seat, she buckled herself in and set the keys down on the driver's seat. She waited for a minute until Anthony joined her, getting in the driver's side.

"So, you have an idea of some things you want to do at the park this week?" asked Anthony as he started the car, backed out of the garage and hit the remote, shutting the door after backing out.

"Yeah, so there's a couple shows I want to see. And the firework displays one of the nights while we're there."

"Anything else?" asked her dad as he turned right down a private road, heading towards the main road.

"Yeah, I want to check out the water park, too. And get breakfast from the character restaurant. They have crepes that you can get with strawberries, blueberries, peaches, and apple cinnamon. I want to try the apple cinnamon."

"Mmm. That sounds good. I think I'm going to try the blueberry one."

"That was going to be my second pick, too."

"Did you read up on the hotel some?"

"Yeah, they have a big Crystal Coast shop in the lobby on the first floor with plushy dolls, shirts, and all sorts of different things."

"That sounds cool."

"And the waterpark."

"Oh yes, they do have a waterpark."

"They do. So, I'm going to ride some of the rides there, too."

"Well, we'll be sure and bring our swimsuits then."

"Okay. Hey and sorry again that your friend Emily couldn't come along too. I know you would have liked her to come along."

"It's fine. Getting to go with you and Mom makes me happy too," said Samantha as she smiled and looked at her dad.

"Love you, honey. I hope we all have a good time."

"Love you too, Dad."

"Are you all packed too?"

"Yeah, I'm going to pack tonight after dinner."

"Will Mom be helping you pack too?"

"Yeah, she said she would. Then we can pack the car tonight and be ready to go to the airport in the morning. What time are we leaving in the morning?"

"Early. I want to leave the house by 6:30 AM. We can stop and grab some breakfast sandwiches before we go to the airport. Our flight leaves at 10:30, so I'd like to be there by 8:00 to find parking in the garage. Plus, that'll give us plenty of time to drop off our luggage, print our tickets, and get through security."

"We could just get breakfast at the airport?"

"No. Food at the airport costs twice as much as it does outside the airport. We can just stop and grab some fast food in the morning somewhere. McDonald's, Burger King, or wherever," said her dad as he pulled into the parking lot of the pizza shop.

"Can I bring something while we wait and for the flight too?"

"Bring something?"

"Ya. Like a book? Or my video game?"

"Oh. Sure, I don't see why not."

Anthony parked the car and got out. Walking into the pizza shop, he came back out a few minutes later with two pizza boxes in hand.

"Here, hang onto them for me. But don't eat them yet," said Anthony, handing Samantha the pizzas.

"Okay, Dad," she said, taking the boxes from him.

She held the boxes in place as her dad got back in and started the car back up.

"Well, I hope you have a good time, honey. Your mom and I have been talking about going to Crystal Coast Kingdom for the longest time now. We figured you would like it."

"I love it. I can't wait to see what it's like there," said Samantha.

On the way back home, Samantha talked about how excited she was about the trip and seeing the Crystal Coast Kingdom for the first time in her life. To ride all the rides and experience the new water park, shops, shows, food, and evening fireworks. She was looking forward to it all.

In no time, they made it back home, and Samantha helped carry the pizzas inside with her father, setting them down on the kitchen counter.

"I'm going to go upstairs and let your mom know we're home, honey. Can you start setting the table and get the drinks out of the fridge, too?"

"Do you want ranch sauce for your pizza, Dad?" asked Samantha.

"No, thank you, honey. I need to cut back on sauce and the calories I get from it."

"Okay, Dad."

Anthony walked upstairs to let Elizabeth know that they were home while Samantha set the table. Once the table was set, she didn't wait for her parents to come downstairs as she took her plate over to the kitchen counter and pulled out a couple of slices of pizza from her pizza box. She walked back over and sat at the table and started eating when Anthony walked back down the stairs.

"Your mom will be down in a minute. She's just drying off and putting her pajamas on. You want something to drink, honey?" asked her dad as he touched the back of her head, rubbing his hand down her hair.

"Oh, yeah, root beer."

"Nice. Root beer is a good drink for pizza," he said as he walked over to the refrigerator and pulled out the two-liter bottle.

"I always liked orange soda with my pizza," said Anthony as he reached in and grabbed the orange soda. "And your mom, she always just likes regular soda."

Anthony walked two bottles over to the kitchen table. He opened the root beer, which hissed as it released built-up carbon dioxide gas. He poured the glasses of soda and served them before helping himself to some pizza. Anthony had always liked deep-dish pie. Especially Chicago-style deep-dish pizza. It felt more like a meal to him than just a regular slice of pizza. When he finished serving himself a slice of deep dish on his plate, Elizabeth had made her way downstairs. Anthony looked up and saw his wife walking towards the dinner table.

"Hey hon, you want some cola to drink with your pizza?" he asked.

"Oh yes, please."

"With ice cubes?"

"Yes, please."

Anthony went to the fridge and pulled out the bottle of cola for Elizabeth and set it down on the counter. He grabbed a glass from the cupboard and filled it with ice from the freezer and poured her a glass of cola. Elizabeth took her plate and walked over to the pizza. Grabbing a couple of slices for herself, she went back to the table and sat down. Anthony brought over the bottle of soda, sitting it down in front of her along with her glass of ice-cold cola.

"Thank you, honey," said Elizabeth as Anthony sat down to start eating pizza too.

They ate pizza that night and spent time together as a family. After dinner, they did the dishes and packed their luggage. When they had finished packing, they took their luggage downstairs to the Suburban in the garage and loaded it. Afterward, they went back inside and played board games at the dining room table for a couple of hours together until they wore themselves out and all three retired for the evening, anticipating a long day of travel from Chicago to Miami tomorrow. Samantha spent a few minutes picking out some clothes to wear tomorrow, setting them aside on her dresser. When she finished picking her clothes, she crawled into bed and fell asleep almost instantly.

*   *   *   *

"Honey, it's time to wake up," said a voice in her bedroom.

Samantha drifted back to reality from the dream she had been having. As she started to get oriented to the bedroom, she looked and saw her mom in the doorway with the hallway light on, shining brightly into her room.

"What time is it?" asked Samantha.

"5:30 honey. Time to get up and get in the shower. Your dad is in our bathroom shower. But we're leaving here in an hour, so get up and jump in the shower and get dressed," said Elizabeth.

"I'm still tired," she replied to her mom.

"You can sleep on the plane, come on. Up," she said, flipping the light switch on in her bedroom.

Bright white light covered every surface of the bedroom. Samantha grunted as she pulled the covers over her head.

"I'll be back in 5 minutes; if you're not up by then, I'm going to be upset, Sam."

"I'll be up," she said from under the covers.

Elizabeth left the light on in Samantha's room as she went back to her bedroom. Samantha uncovered her face and yawned. She stretched her arms above her head and then removed the covers. Swinging her legs out of bed, she sat along the side of her bed and prepared for the day. She used the bathroom, brushed her teeth, took a shower, and got dressed all by herself like her mom had asked. When she finished changing, she put her pajamas into the clothing hamper, as well as her bathrobe, and then proceeded to pack her backpack with a couple of books and a small portable game system that she could play at the airport or on the plane. She also packed her charging cable for her phone and portable game, as well as a set of small headphones that she could listen to her devices with too. As she was zipping up her backpack, her dad walked into her bedroom.

"Hey honey, is there anything you want to take with you today?" asked Anthony.

"Yeah, I just packed up my backpack to carry on the plane," said Samantha.

"Oh, good. Your mom is just taking a quick shower, and when she finishes and gets dressed, then we're going to start heading to the airport."

"Sounds good, Dad."

"Hey, are you excited today?"

"Excited, yes. Also tired."

"I know, honey. You can sleep on the plane," said Anthony as he left her bedroom with her backpack in hand.

Samantha left her room, shutting the light off behind her. She carefully stepped down the stairs and walked into the living room. Sitting down in a recliner, she started to fall asleep again when she heard her mom coming down the stairs.

"Hey, Sam. Are you ready to go?"

"Yeah, Mom. Just waiting on you," said Sam as she leaned up and got out of the recliner.

"Well, I'm ready to go. I'll try to convince your dad to stop for breakfast on the way to the airport."

"I don't think you'll have to convince him too much. I think his plan was to stop for breakfast sandwiches."

"Oh, good. Depending on where we go, I may just get a coffee there. Or maybe get a coffee at the airport."

"Can I have a coffee this morning?"

"You can have a small one," she said as they both walked into the kitchen.

"Sam, have you got everything you need? Want to walk through your bedroom one more time to make sure?"

"I got everything I need, Mom. I'm good."

"Okay. Is your dad in the car already?"

"I think I did see him go into the garage a little while ago."

"He's probably waiting in the car then."

They shut the lights off around the house, then got into the car in the garage, where Anthony was waiting for them.

"Hey, hurry up it's almost 6:30," said Anthony.

"We're stopping for breakfast, yes?" asked Elizabeth.

"Yes, yes. Probably McDonalds. Get some Sausage McMuffins."

"Great. Sounds good, come on, honey, get in the back," said Elizabeth as she walked around the front of the suburban and got in the passenger side.

"Did you remember to let the Howards know to keep an eye on the place?" asked Elizabeth.

"Yes, I texted Frank and let him know that we were heading out and if they could keep an eye on the place. All the automatic lights are set to turn on around 8:00 PM and then shut off around one in the morning, too."

Samantha opened the door behind the driver's side and got into the back seat. Anthony opened the garage door and started up the Suburban. When the door was fully opened, he backed out of the garage and shut the door and waited in the driveway to see that the door had shut completely and remained shut. When the door closed, he backed out onto the road and started his drive to the airport.

Chapter 3: O'Hare International Airport

"Oh, there's a spot," said Elizabeth, pointing out an open parking spot in the parking garage at O'Hare International Airport.

Anthony parked the Suburban, and they all got out.

"Okay, you two. I'm going to get one of the luggage carts. Sam, make sure the garbage from the breakfast sandwich wrappers this morning are gathered and thrown away, okay?"

"Okay, Dad."

"I'll be back in a minute, hon."

"Okay."

Samantha got back into the Suburban and picked up the wrappers from the seats, putting them into the paper bag the sandwiches had come in. When she had gathered the last bit of garbage from the suburban, she jumped back out and shut the door behind her. Samantha walked the garbage over to a nearby can and threw it away. As she was walking back to the car, her dad was coming with the luggage cart.

"Thanks for doing that, Sam," said Anthony.

"No problem, Dad."

"You want to put your luggage on the bottom of the cart, hon?" asked Elizabeth.

"Yeah, we can do that. Then your stuff. Then Sams. Samantha, do you want to put your backpack on?" asked Anthony as he reached into the back and grabbed her backpack, handing it to her.

"Yes, thanks, Dad."

Together, they gathered their luggage and organized it on the cart. Once they were loaded on, Samantha handed her bags to Elizabeth.

"Oh, thank you, honey. We'll put yours on top here," she said, picking up Samantha's luggage and setting it on top of the other cases.

"Okay. Anything else you guys think we need from the suburban? Liz, you want to take one more look around in the car?" asked Anthony.

"No, I think we've got everything we need," said Elizabeth.

"Alright, I think we're good here then," said Anthony, as he locked the Suburban with his remote key fob, stuffed the keys into his pocket and turned and started pushing the cart with all the luggage on it.

"You want me to walk ahead and see if I can find where the elevator up to check-in is?" asked Elizabeth.

"I think it's down the way here, and around the corner. Yeah, you can walk ahead for a minute and make sure."

"I'll go with you, Mom," said Samantha.

"Okay, stay close and watch out for traffic," said Elizabeth as they took off together, leaving Anthony pushing the cart behind for a moment as they went ahead to see where they needed to go.

When they got far enough ahead, they saw that the elevators were just around the corner of the main lane in the garage.

"Anthony! It is down here. You need some help pushing?"

"No, it's fine. Go ahead and hit the button for the elevator, and I'll be there in just a minute."

Elizabeth walked over to the button on the wall, hitting the button next to the sign that read *main terminal/check-in desks*. She and Samantha stepped back and waited to see which one of the eight elevators would be coming down to pick them up, just as Anthony turned the corner and pushed the cart towards them. The elevator doors opened, and Elizabeth and Samantha quickly ran into it. Holding the doors open with their hands, Anthony followed close behind with the luggage cart. Once all three were inside the elevator, the doors closed, and the elevator went up a few floors before stopping.

The doors squeaked as they opened onto a busy airport terminal. Chicago O'Hare International Airport was a bustling hub of activity, with a constant stream of travelers navigating through its busy terminals. The airport saw many people moving about at any given time, making it a lively and vibrant space. From families embarking on vacations to business travelers rushing to catch their flights, O'Hare was always abuzz with energy. Numerous shops, restaurants, and amenities catered to the diverse needs of every passenger who walked in and out. The airport offered a wide range of services to ensure a comfortable and convenient travel experience for everyone, including Samantha and her family as they exited the elevator and made their way into the terminal.

"Anthony, are we looking for Delta?" asked Elizabeth.

"Yes," he said, carefully navigating the cart through the crowd of travelers.

Elizabeth looked up and down the main aisle of all the different airliner signs when she finally saw the Delta logo a few desks up from where they were.

"I see Delta, Anthony. It's up a way still."

"Jesus Christ, of course it is," said Anthony under his breath, as he started to get frustrated.

"Want me to go and print out our boarding passes?" she asked.

"Yes, go ahead. I'll be there in a minute, hon," he said as he started pushing the cart through the terminal.

Elizabeth and Samantha walked on ahead until they got to Delta and used the computers available to check in and print out their boarding tickets. When they had finished printing them, Anthony finally caught up, sweat forming on his brow

"Okay, I printed all three of our boarding passes out. Let's get in line to check our luggage."

Elizabeth kept the boarding passes together as they got in line and waited for the desk clerk to help them check their bags on. It didn't take long as the clerk ushered them to the counter and spent a little time checking in their luggage and sticking the tags on it, indicating the luggage was flying to Miami, Florida. Once all the luggage was checked in for them, they took the cart away. Much to the delight of Anthony, who didn't have to push the damn heavy thing anymore.

They entered the security line for Terminal B and waited for over half an hour in line until it was their turn to go through security. Removing metal jewelry, belts, shoes and their backpacks and the contents of their backpacks, each family member went through security efficiently without any hitches. Once they were through security and dressed again, they made their way to the airport flight screen and located their flight to Miami. Delta flight DL1941, departing from terminal C31 on time. Boarding was about to start in half an hour.

"This is great! We have plenty of time to walk to terminal C31 before they board," said Anthony.

"Can we stop by one of the tourist shops and get a couple of magazines to read on the flight?" asked Elizabeth.

"Sure. Fine by me. Come on, Sam. Don't get left behind," said Anthony as he and Elizabeth started walking to the Concord C.

Samantha followed close behind them. The family wandered through the terminal, moving in and out of the heavy crowds who were traveling for summer vacation. Samantha looked up and counted down each gate as they walked by. From C1 to C2, all the way to about C25 when her parents both stopped for a moment.

"Oh, here is one of those shops," said Elizabeth.

"Honey, we're going to go inside. You want to come in too?" Anthony asked Samantha.

"Oh, no, I'll wait for you guys out here," replied Samantha.

Both Anthony and Elizabeth walked inside the shop, disappearing into the store among the crowd who were purchasing last-minute snacks, drinks, and books or magazines. Samantha waited by the front when a small rack of books caught her eye. She walked over to the books, picking some up and reading the front covers and then the back covers.

"Hmm. Solipsism. Sounds creepy," she said as she turned the book over to read the back cover to learn what it was about.

"What's a young girl like you looking at horror books like that?" asked a voice next to her.

Samantha looked over and saw a balding, middle-aged man with beard stubble on his face that looked as if he had shaved yesterday morning. He wore glasses that appeared to be bifocals and wore a purple windbreaker jacket and old faded blue jeans. He carried no luggage with him. Not even a carry-on. Samantha felt uneasy around the man, the way he looked at her and analyzed her while she was looking at the book.

"I like scary books, I guess," she replied.

"Oh yeah, so do I." He picked up a book from the shelf, too. "Do you like pirate stories? This one, Black Flags, looks like it's about pirates. Very exciting," he said as his face contorted as he smiled and his eyes bulged out a little, enhanced by the magnification of his glasses.

"I'm sorry. I'm sure your folks have told you not to talk to strangers. So let me introduce myself to you. I'm Carl. What's your name?" Asked the man.

"Samantha," she said.

"Samantha. That's a pretty name. Pleasure to meet you. Where are you from?"

"Chicago."

"Oh. I'm from Rhinelander. Do you know where that is?"

"Wisconsin?"

"Yeah, Wisconsin. Northern Wisconsin. Where are you headed?" asked Carl.

"We're flying to Miami this morning."

"Oh, very nice. I'm flying to San Antonio. Meeting my brother in Texas at a family reunion for the week."

"Why don't you have any luggage with you?"

"Oh, I checked it on. I don't like carrying a bag with me. Plus, I still have a lot of clothes back home in Texas, so I really didn't have to pack much in my check-on either."

"Oh. When do you fly out to Texas?"

"Oh, later this afternoon. I think I'll have lunch and then head over to my terminal. How about you?"

"We're flying out in a couple of hours."

"Oh, around 10:30?"

"Yeah."

"Oh. Well, I hope you have a good flight. It was a pleasure meeting you, Samantha. Safe travels," he said, smiling awkwardly at her again.

"Yeah, you too."

Carl set the book back down on the shelf and walked away, leaving Samantha by herself at the bookrack in front of the store. She put the book back on the shelf, then walked into the store and found her parents, who were standing in line.

"Honey, do you want something to have for a snack on the flight?" asked Elizabeth, holding a couple of magazines in her hand.

"Umm, yeah, can I get a Twix, please?"

"Sure. I'll grab one for you. You want anything else?"

"No, just that is fine."

"How about some gum?"

"No."

"Small bag of chips?"

"Do they have Doritos?"

"I think I see bags of Doritos up there."

"I'll take the nacho cheese ones if they have them."

"You want something to drink too?"

"I'll take a cola."

"Okay, grab yourself a cola too."

Samantha went over and got herself a small bottle of cola and brought it back to her mom. After paying for their snacks, magazines, and a book that Anthony got to read, they left the store and proceeded to make their way to gate C-31 in the terminal. It didn't take them long to get there, where they found some seats to sit at to wait. Samantha pulled out her portable game system from her backpack and began playing it as her parents talked for a minute before they started reading the materials they had bought from the shop.

Meanwhile, over at gate C29, a balding man with glasses, in a purple windbreaker and faded blue jeans, spoke with the attendant at the counter and changed his flight ticket from San Antonio to DL1941, the flight from Chicago to Miami.

Chapter 4: Miami, Florida

"Ladies and gentlemen, this is your captain speaking. We'd like to thank you for flying Delta Air Lines Flight DL1941 nonstop from Chicago, Illinois, to Miami, Florida. The total flight time will be about four and a half hours, close to twelve hundred miles of distance covered in that stretch. I suspect that we're going to experience some strong headwinds from the east coast as we're flying by the Carolinas, and if we do, I will turn on the overhead seatbelt light and ask that you all return to your seats if you are up, and limit walking about the cabin of the plane during that stretch of the flight. It should take about 15 minutes from the ground to reach maximum altitude on our flight. The weather in Miami when we land says that it should be sunny skies and great summer weather at the beach. You guys picked a good time to head to Florida. Please fasten your seatbelts as we'll be taking off here momentarily. Flight attendants, please prepare the cabin for takeoff."

Samantha put away her portable game system and buckled up, sitting in a row with her parents, excited for take-off. The flight attendants walked up and down the aisles, checking to make sure everyone's seatbelts were buckled in, and trays were stored in the upright position. They then demonstrated what to do in the event of an emergency before they returned to their respective seats and buckled themselves in for take-off, too. It wasn't long after that, when the plane backed up from the gate and onto the tarmac of O'Hare International Airport. It paused for a moment before the plane lurched forward, taxiing up the tarmac to its starting position on the runway. When the plane was in position, it roared to life and, with a powerful surge, it accelerated up the runway. The wheels lifted off the ground, retracting into the body of the plane from underneath, and in an exhilarating moment, it broke free from the earth's grasp, soaring into the brightly lit, late morning sky.

The world below them faded away as the plane entered the clouds, and the adventure of the flight began, filled with endless possibilities and the thrill of exploration.

A short time later, when the plane was at its maximum altitude of nearly thirty-five thousand feet, the pilot turned off the seatbelt sign and got on the overhead radio to address the passengers again.

"Good morning, this is your captain speaking again. We are now at maximum altitude, and you are free to move about the cabin as needed. I would suspect that we will hit that turbulence here in approximately a couple of hours, so be looking for the fasten seatbelts light on the overhead again and please return to your seats then and limit moving about the cabin. Otherwise, you are now free to move about the cabin."

"Dad, can I use the bathroom in the back?" asked Samantha.

"Sure, you need me to get out of my seat?"

"No, I can get by," she replied as she took her headphones off, unbuckled her seatbelt and stood up.

She managed to get past Anthony's knees and out into the aisle. Walking back to the bathroom, she stopped at the door just as someone walked out. Samantha opened the door, went in, and handled her business. When she was finished, she washed her hands in the sink, dried them off, and exited the bathroom. She opened the door into someone who was on the other side, and as she was coming out, Samantha was about to apologize when she looked up and saw the same man there at the door that she had seen in the airport terminal back in Chicago.

"Oh, hey. Samantha, right?" said the man.

"Yeah. Carl, wasn't it?"

"Yeah, you remembered my name."

"What are you doing here?"

"Oh, I'm flying to Miami, then hopping on another flight to fly to San Antonio. The airport asked me if I would be interested in changing flights because the direct flight to San Antonio was overbooked, so they put me on this one for a slight refund. It doesn't matter to me too much. It's free money back."

"Oh, I see."

"Are you here with your parents?"

"Yeah, they're up at my seat right now."

"Cool. Well, hey, it's good seeing you again. I hope you enjoy your flight. I'm sorry to cut our visit short again, but I really need to use the bathroom. I should have gone before we left Chicago."

"Oh, okay. Have a good flight too," said Samantha as she turned and walked away, back up the aisle to her seat.

Carl stood there for a moment, his eyes behind thick-lensed glasses watching her walk away, before he opened the door to the bathroom and went inside.

Samantha returned to her seat in the aisle with her parents, who were both now reading their magazines and books. She wiggled past her dad's knees and sat back down in her seat.

"Dad," she said.

"Yes, honey?"

"What book are you reading?"

"Oh, The Dark Side of the Moon. It's a scary alien story. Sounded interesting at the bookstore in the airport, and you know how I like scary stories."

"Yeah. I'm going to start watching my movie again."

She reached into the pocket of the seat in front of her and took out her headphones. Putting them on, she hit the play on the small screen in the back of the headrest of the seat in front of her and resumed watching her cartoon movie. Samantha watched the movie for a bit before she started to fall asleep in the seat, as her head fell to the side of her shoulder.

"Honey, do you want your neck pillow?" asked Elizabeth.

"No, I'm fine, Mom," she replied as she jolted awake, but only for a moment as she drifted off into sleep again.

When she opened her eyes, she looked up at the screen of the small television. Her movie was over, and the screen was dark. She looked over at her mom, who was looking out the window. She glanced over at her father, who was still reading in his book, but nearly halfway through the book already. She leaned over to where her mom was, looking out the window and noticing that the ground was getting closer and closer now.

"Whoa, wait. Where are we?"

"Oh, hey Sam. You woke up. You slept through the whole flight. We're starting to land here in Miami," she replied.

"Are you serious? I slept the whole flight?"

"You sure did. You were up early, honey. Your dad and I just decided to let you rest."

"How long until we're on the ground?"

"Oh, probably in about ten minutes. The captain of the plane said we would be landing in half an hour, and that was about twenty minutes ago."

"Cool."

"Hey, you woke up," said Anthony.

"Yeah, how is your book?" she asked.

"Scary, and pretty good. I'm going to stop at the end of that chapter though, now that we're landing."

As the plane descended through the white, fluffy clouds, the young girl continued to look out the window, her eyes sparkling with excitement at nearly landing and starting her vacation. She watched as the sprawling city of Miami drew closer; a patchwork of vibrant colors and sun-soaked beaches in the distance and pristine blue ocean waters. With a gentle thud, the aircraft landed on the runway, sending a thrill of anticipation coursing through her. The tires rolled smoothly along the runway as the plane taxied through the tarmac and towards the gate to the airport.

"Crystal Kingdom, here we come!" She whispered to herself, a huge grin of excitement spreading across her face, ready to embark on a new adventure in this sun-kissed paradise of Florida.

The plane came to a stop at the gate as it parked by the exit ramp for passengers to disembark.

"Ladies and gentlemen, this is your captain speaking from the flight deck. I'm pleased to announce that we have safely landed in beautiful Miami, Florida. As we exit the aircraft, you can look forward to experiencing the nice, warm, sunny weather that this vibrant city is known for. Give us a few minutes to get the door open, to leave the plane and to unpack the luggage bay too. When you reach the luggage pickup for checked bags, go to luggage bay thirteen. Your luggage will be waiting to be picked up there in the next ten to fifteen minutes. On behalf of Delta Airlines, I would like to extend our heartfelt thanks for choosing to fly with us today. We appreciate your business and hope you have a wonderful time here in Miami. Safe travels to you all."

The passengers waited for a moment as Samantha sat as patiently as she could in her seat. Anthony got up and stood out in the main aisle, opening the overhead storage and taking out his carry-on luggage, handing it to Elizabeth and then to Samantha, before he grabbed his carry-on. A few moments later, there was a bang toward the front, and Anthony could see that passengers were starting to exit the plane.

"Okay, looks like they are starting to leave the plane now, you guys," he said.

They cleared out of the plane as a family. Anthony led the way as they walked down the boarding bridge into the Miami International Airport terminal. It took almost a full minute of walking, but they finally made it and were now standing in the center of the airport. Passengers swarmed around them, moving quickly to and from different terminals.

"The baggage pickup is this way," said Anthony as he pointed out the sign that indicated luggage pickup was to the left.

Elizabeth and Samantha followed Anthony as he walked down the terminal, passing gate after gate until he approached an exit from the terminal area. After passing the red line, they made their way to an escalator that took them down a level into the baggage claim area. They found luggage pickup bay thirteen and waited for a few minutes before an audible buzzer sounded, accompanied by a red flashing light as the conveyor belt started and the luggage made its way down on the conveyor belt. One by one, luggage of different shapes, sizes, and colors ran down the conveyor belt until Samantha spotted her luggage coming to her on the conveyor line. She grabbed her things from the belt, followed by Elizabeth, who grabbed her luggage, and finally one of the last pieces of luggage that came down the conveyor belt was Anthony's. He grabbed his check on bag and stepped away from the belt as people were grabbing their bags from the belt, too. The three then stepped to the side of the baggage claim area and sat down for a moment. Anthony pulled out his phone and glanced at it momentarily.

"Okay, Liz, it says on here that the shuttle to Crystal Mountain picks up passengers at parking lot ten. The reservation here in the email says we need to call their shuttle service to notify them that we've arrived at the airport. Can you call them? I'll read you the number and give you the reservation number they'll need."

"Sure, hon. What's the number?" asked Elizabeth.

Samantha reached into her backpack and grabbed a couple of pieces of gum to chew on as Anthony gave the number to the shuttle service and Elizabeth called them. Anthony then took off to collect a luggage trolley in the baggage claim area. The phone rang a couple of times before it was answered by a guest service representative of the shuttle service.

"Good afternoon, and thank you for calling Crystal Mountain Resort transportation and shuttle services. My name is Tracy. How can I help you?"

"Hi, good afternoon. My family and I have a shuttle reservation made for pickup at the airport this afternoon, to be taken to the Crystal Mountain Resort hotel," said Elizabeth over the phone.

Samantha stood and watched as people went to and from around baggage claim. Kids with their parents who weren't paying attention to them while they too were on the phone making phone calls to what she assumed were shuttles and rides too. Anthony was also coming back with a baggage cart.

"Okay. So you have shuttles arriving every half hour to parking lot C1. Where is parking lot C1? Hey, I'm going to put you on speakerphone so my husband can hear you, too."

Elizabeth brought the phone down from her ear and looked at the screen. Tapping the screen, she activated the speakerphone setting.

"Can you hear me?" asked Elizabeth.

"Yes, ma'am," said a middle-aged female voice on the other end of the line.

"Okay great, now can you explain to us where parking lot C1 is?"

"Of course, and are you in the baggage claim area or at the entrance to the airport?"

"Baggage claim."

"Okay, so you are going to take the escalator up to the next level and cross over the sky bridge that connects the parking garage to the airport. Once you are in the parking garage, there are going to be some elevators on your left. Take the elevator up a level to the C lot in the parking garage. When you step out of the elevators, you will see some signs there that will direct you to the shuttle pickup zone. It will be on the left of the elevators. You're going to wait there for the shuttle to pick you up, which there should be a couple on their way there in about twenty minutes. A couple just completed a pickup about ten minutes ago, so make your way over to lot C and wait at the pickup zone, and we'll have some more shuttles there in just a bit."

"Okay, we can do that. Thank you for the directions, too."

"No problem at all, ma'am. We'll see you here in a little bit."

"Sounds good, thank you. Goodbye."

Elizabeth hung up her phone and looked up at Anthony.

"Twenty minutes, we've gotta get going. Sam, can you put your luggage on the cart for me?" asked Elizabeth.

Samantha picked up her checked bag, setting it onto the bottom of the luggage cart. Anthony picked up both Elizabeth and his bag, setting them into the luggage cart as well. Samantha took her backpack off and set it on the cart, too.

"Okay, you guys ready to go?" asked Anthony.

"I'll go grab the elevator," said Elizabeth.

"You guys want to take the escalator, and I'll just take the elevator?"

"No, it's fine. We can take the elevator with you, too."

Each step felt like a mission at this point to Samantha as the family pushed through the throng of travelers in baggage claim. Elizabeth reached the elevator first, hitting the button to summon the elevator to go up a level to the second floor. With a chime, the doors opened, and they hopped in. The door closed behind them and the elevator roared to life as they ascended one more floor, a leap closer to the thrills that awaited them on their vacation. It was all a blur as they rushed across the skywalk to the parking garage together. Once in the garage, they turned left and saw the elevators that the theme park's service worker was telling them about. They walked over and pushed the button to the set of elevators there to go up a level to the C section. The elevator chimed and slowly opened in front of them. The family got on with a couple of other folks who were going up, too. They barely made it before the door closed in on them.

"We're sorry about that. We just needed to go up too," said the older woman, standing beside an older man.

"Perfectly fine, let me try to give you some more room to get in," said Anthony as he nudged the cart up against the back wall of the elevator some.

"Are you folks here on vacation too?" asked the woman as the elevator doors closed.

"Yes, we are," said Elizabeth.

"Very nice, so are we. We're from Seattle," said the woman. "My name is Bev; this is my husband, Marvin."

"Pleasure to meet you, I'm Anthony, this is my wife, Elizabeth. And our daughter, Samantha."

"Pleased to meet you all," said the older man.

"We're from Chicago," said Elizabeth.

"Oh, very nice. I have a younger sister who has lived in Rockford, Illinois, with her husband for almost thirty years now. We'll have to go back there in a couple of years for their thirtieth anniversary."

"Oh, Rockford. Yes, that's just to the east of us. What brings you folks to Miami?"

"We're meeting our daughter and her husband and our grandchildren at the Crystal Mountain Resort. We're heading up to the C lot to catch the shuttle."

"No kidding, that's where we are going too. We're here for a full week on summer vacation," said Elizabeth.

"Oh wow, that sounds fun! Yeah, we're here for about a week too, and then we'll head back to Seattle."

The elevator doors opened, and everyone got off the elevator and walked over to the shuttle pickup area.

"Well, I think this is where the shuttle pickup is for the resort hotel," said the older woman.

"That's how the operator on the phone had described it too. Look, there's a sign for Crystal Mountain too," said Anthony, pointing out the sign close by the elevators.

"No, that's it. This is where the shuttle pickup is," said Elizabeth. "I suppose we just wait here now."

"Well, I'm glad that we bumped into you here," said the old woman. "Are you folks staying at the resort as well or at a hotel nearby?"

"We're staying at the resort for the week."

"Very nice. I hear that there are great places to eat on the grounds there."

"Absolutely. We're looking forward to the fireworks displays in the evenings. We'll go check that out tonight too," said Anthony.

"I hear that it's breathtaking. Every evening at 10:00 PM, they shoot off fireworks over their lagoon there. Supposed to be a great show every night."

The two families continued talking about the resort when a couple of other families came and waited along with them. Then another family with two younger boys came and waited in the waiting area for the shuttles. Everyone got to know everyone else, sharing their excitement about going to the resort. In a short amount of time, three white vans arrived at the shuttle pickup zone.

"I thought they said there would only be two?" asked Anthony.

"Well, there are a lot of people here waiting to be picked up. Maybe they knew that and sent the extra van down," replied Elizabeth.

Everyone got in line and started boarding the shuttle. Samantha and her parents boarded the first van that had parked in the pickup area. The drivers helped all the passengers load their luggage in the back of the vans. After the last of the passengers were loaded, the first van took off with Samantha and her family. A few moments later, when the driver got into the second van, it took off for the Crystal Mountain resort.

The driver of the third van was in the process of closing the back door to the shuttle. He turned and started to walk around the side of the van to the driver's side of the shuttle when a hand grabbed his shoulder from behind. The man turned around to see a middle-aged man, balding, with some beard stubble on his face that looked as if he had shaved yesterday morning. He wore bifocals and a purple windbreaker jacket and old faded blue jeans. He carried no luggage with him. Not even a backpack.

"Excuse me, sir. Is this shuttle going to the Crystal Mountain Resort?" asked the man.

"Yes, it is," replied the driver.

"You got room for one more?"

"I do. Do you have anyone joining you today?"

"Just myself."

"Okay, any luggage?"

"No luggage either."

"No luggage?" asked the driver.

"Yes, sir. No luggage."

"Alright. The front seat is still open unless you want to crawl your way into the back seat?"

"I can take the front seat."

"Let me grab the door for you."

"It's alright, I can get it," said the man as he turned and walked around the side of the van to the passenger door.

The driver then turned the corner of the van and got into the driver's side of the van. The last passenger got into the front passenger seat of the van.

"Everyone buckled in?" asked the driver.

In unison, all the passengers in the van said, "Yes."

The driver stepped on the brake, put the van into drive, on the way to the Crystal Mountain Resort.

Chapter 5: Crystal Mountain Resort and Theme Park

The sun descended from the highest point in the sky, painting the horizon with hues of gold and orange as the shuttle made its way down the winding road towards the resort. The families on board each one of the shuttles were humming with excitement, their faces lit up with anticipation for the fun they were about to have. Children in the vans pressed their noses against the windows, gazing wide-eyed at the lush greenery and sparkling waters that unfolded before them there at the resort.

"Look! There's the pool!" Samantha exclaimed, her voice a melody of joy that echoed through the shuttle.

Laughter filled the air, and all the parents in the shuttle vans exchanged knowing smiles with one another, reminiscing about their own childhood vacations that they would take with their parents. As the shuttle approached the grand entrance to the hotel, a collective gasp escaped the group. Towering palm trees swayed gently in the evening breeze, and the sound of waves lapping against the shore was like a siren's call. The vibrant colors of the Crystal Mountain Hotel and Theme Park facade splashed against the backdrop of a brilliant sunset, promising unforgettable memories to come.

"Welcome to paradise, you guys!" the driver announced with a grin.

The families erupted in cheers, excitement bubbling over as they prepared to step into a world of leisure and joy for their vacation. The shuttle parked in front of the hotel, and its doors swung wide open, ready to unleash a wave of adventure to each family.

Samantha jumped out of the van, followed by her mother and father. The other families got out of the van as well, and everyone walked into the hotel lobby together. The driver assisted in unloading luggage out of the back of the van, as Anthony went and grabbed a luggage cart from the front of the lobby in the hotel. He loaded up the luggage onto the cart and pushed it just inside past the doors, where he met up with Elizabeth and Samantha, who were gawking at the architecture of the resort hotel.

After walking inside the lobby, the families were met by Crystal Mountain Theme Park characters who welcomed them to their vacations. The lobby was of an open-air design. Beautiful arches and architecture allowed the cool wind to flow through the hotel's lobby. A water fountain stood in the center of the large waiting area by the front desk, where tourists would make their wishes and toss copper pennies in, in hopes that their wishes would come true. Local and tropical plants in planters were scattered throughout the lobby as each family approached the front desk to check into the hotel.

"Dad, are we going to get some dinner tonight?" asked Samantha.

"Ya, we'll try getting some dinner at the Chinese restaurant here in the resort. Your mom talked about trying to have dinner there when we were on the plane, and you were asleep," said Anthony.

"Do they have sweet and sour chicken?"

"Yeah, I'm sure they have that there."

"Great, I love sweet and sour chicken."

"I know you do."

"Hi, welcome to Crystal Mountain Resort and Theme Park. Do you have a reservation with us?" asked the front desk clerk.

"Yes, we do. It should be under the last name of Owen," said Anthony as he took his wallet out of his back pocket, setting it on the counter and pulling out his driver's license and credit card.

"Owen. Oh yes, here it is. Anthony and Elizabeth, yes?"

"That's right, ma'am."

"Looks like you guys will be here through Sunday and checking out Monday morning on the 16th?"

"Yes, that's right," said Anthony.

"Okay, so it looks like everything is paid for already. We just need a credit card for incidentals to put on the room. So, if you want to charge meals to your room, for instance, then we'll have a card to put it on."

"You can put it on this card," said Anthony, handing his American Express card to her.

"Thank you," she said and took the card and entered it into the machine at the counter.

"Okay, if you can go ahead and sign your name on the pad with the magnetic pen and then hit the green okay button below."

Anthony signed his name on the pad, and did what she said, hitting the green button to accept his signature.

"Okay, thank you for that. How many key cards will you guys be needing?" asked the clerk.

"Three please. One for each of us."

The clerk activated the three keycards and handed them out to Anthony, Elizabeth, and Samantha.

"Okay, I would like to extend a warm welcome to Crystal Mountain Resort and Theme Park. Our establishment offers a range of amenities designed to enhance your stay, including complimentary breakfast, a fitness center, and a business lounge. There are also several restaurants on the resort site, so you won't need to leave the resort at any point for any reason unless you choose to do so. Should you require any assistance during your visit, please do not hesitate to contact the front desk, as we are here to ensure your experience is both comfortable and enjoyable. You can contact us by the phones in the room, stopping by the front desk, or even if you would like to download the Crystal Mountain Theme Park app for your smartphone, you can do that too and connect with us there. If you have any problems with the room, then please notify us, and if we can't fix the problem, then we will be happy to move you to a different room of equal value that will meet your needs. If a room of equal value is not available, then we will automatically upgrade you to the next-level room up, without an extra charge. Thank you for choosing Crystal Mountain Resort and Theme Park, and we hope you enjoy your stay with us."

"Thank you, ma'am. We will," said Elizabeth.

"Would you like help taking your luggage up to your room?" the clerk asked.

"Actually, yes, that would be great. I'm tired of lugging our bags around everywhere we go," said Anthony with an exhausted look on his face.

The front desk clerk chuckled to herself. "No worries at all, I will call one of our bellhops to the front desk, and they will help assist you up to your room on the seventh floor here in a few minutes."

"Thank you, ma'am. Okay you guys, let's get out of the way for the next person," said Anthony, as he moved his family to the side along with the cart of their luggage and bags.

"So, what's the first thing that you want to do when we get everything up to our room?" Elizabeth asked Samantha.

"Dinner. I'm hungry," she said.

"I agree. Let's check out that Chinese restaurant like we talked about earlier," said Anthony.

"Sounds good to me. Then after that, do you want to walk in the park for a little bit?" asked Elizabeth.

"That sounds good. Maybe we can finish dinner soon enough to get out and see the fireworks tonight."

"That would be awesome!" said Samantha excitedly.

A younger man dressed in a red polo shirt and khaki shorts walked up to them from the front desk.

"Hello, are you the Owen family?" asked the young man.

"Yes, we are. Are you the bellhop?"

"Yes, sir. I'm here to help you upstairs with your luggage."

"Thank you so much for your help," said Elizabeth.

"Yes, I've had to haul all this from home to the airport in Chicago, then from the airport here in Miami to this point here. I'd be happy to get some help."

"Hey, you're on vacation. It's time to relax. You're in the happiest place on earth right now, you shouldn't have to do any more work for the rest of your stay here," said the young man, grabbing the luggage cart and pushing it across the lobby to the resort's elevators.

"Well, we appreciate the help."

"Which floor are you guys going up to?"

"Floor seven. Room 714."

"Oh, 714. That has a nice view of the beach and ocean. My name is Travis, by the way. I'm one of the hops that work here at the resort," he said as he continued to push the luggage cart with the family's luggage through the lobby, towards the elevators.

"Pleased to meet you, Travis. I'm Anthony; this is my wife, Elizabeth. And our daughter, Samantha."

"Hello, pleased to meet you both," said Travis. He stopped in front of the elevators and hit the button on the wall to go up.

"Pleasure to meet you as well."

"If you all need anything during your stay here, you can let me know or any other bellhop here know, and we can take care of things for you. We have maintenance around the clock, twenty-four hours a day. Seven days a week here too."

"That's very reassuring."

"Yeah, and the front desk to the lobby is manned every hour of every day of the year too."

"Even Christmas?"

"Christmas is one of our busiest days here."

The elevator dinged, and a moment later the doors opened in front of Travis.

"Lucky me. Usually, it's one of the other elevators that opens, then we have to try to hurry and get over catching the doors from closing," said the young bellhop as he pushed the luggage cart onto the elevator. Samantha and her parents followed closely behind him.

"So how long are you folks here for?"

"For the whole week and won't be leaving until the following Monday."

"Very nice! Have plans for tonight? The restaurants here are great!" said Travis as he hit the button on the elevator control panel for the seventh floor.

The doors closed, and the elevator started up, rising to the seventh floor of the fifteen-level resort hotel.

"That's good. Do you have any recommendations of places to eat?"

"The Chinese restaurant is great. The Thai restaurant, and then we also have an Italian restaurant just here in the hotel, that are both pretty good too. Then if you're interested in Mexican, there is a nice Mexican restaurant outside the hotel, but there's one here in the theme park too called Mazatlan."

"Sounds good. What do you recommend at the Chinese restaurant?"

"The sweet and sour chicken, with the fried rice. Really, anything you get off the menu is pretty good, but that's my go-to favorite meal from there."

"That's great! That's my favorite!" said Samantha.

"Well, you're in for a real treat then."

The elevator slowed its ascent up the floors until it came to a stop at level seven. The elevator dinged, and then slowly opened, revealing a hallway with bright red carpets and gold decorations on the wall. Pictures of the theme park characters lined each side of the walls, along with decorations on the front of each door.

"Alright, right this way, you guys," said Travis as he pushed the cart off the elevator and onto the floor, leading the excited family to their room for the next week.

"What you folks will like about this room is that it has two separate bedrooms for privacy. Along with a small kitchenette and living room space where you can relax after long days of play. Oh, and I forgot to mention the balcony you can sit out on and enjoy some morning sunrises, too."

"It all sounds great," said Elizabeth, as they stepped in front of room 714.

"Alright, here it is. Samantha, can you open the door to your vacation home for the next week?" asked Travis with a smile on his face.

Samantha removed her key card from the protective sleeve and waved it by the electronic lock on the door. The lock scanned the card, flashed green and unlocked with a click. She reached up and grabbed the handle to the door, opened it, and pushed the door open, revealing a beautiful room painted in bright white color. First, they noticed the spacious two bedrooms, each with their own personality, promising peaceful slumber for everyone. The rooms took on themes from the theme park. Characters were scattered throughout the rooms in pictures and as stuffed animals. Beyond the bedrooms lay a cozy living room, where an inviting electric fireplace flickered beneath a large flat-screen TV perched on the shelf above. The comfortable sofa and armchairs invited them to relax and unwind after a long day of exploring in the park.

But the real surprise was the small but perfectly functional kitchen. Equipped with a refrigerator, microwave, and stovetop, it was a game-changer for families visiting the park. It gave families the opportunity to cook meals in their rooms if they wished to do so.

The crown jewel of the suite, though, was undoubtedly the balcony. Sliding glass doors opened onto a breathtaking panoramic view of Miami Beach and the waves from the Atlantic Ocean, lapping up onto the sand. The turquoise water shimmered under the Florida sun, while white sand stretched as far as the eye could see in both directions. Palm trees swayed gently in the breeze, while people walked up and down the beach line. It was pure, unadulterated paradise.

Entering the room, the family immediately stepped out onto the balcony, breathing in the salty air and soaking up the view. In that moment for them, all the stress and worries of everyday life back home melted away.

"So, what do you think, Sam?" asked Anthony.

"I think it's awesome! Can we move here?" she asked.

Her parents laughed.

"Well, do you think we should get ready and go downstairs and find the Chinese restaurant?" asked Anthony.

"Yeah, I think so. I'm hungry," said Elizabeth.

"So am I," said Samantha.

"Alright, there you go," said the young bellhop, as he unloaded the last of the bags onto one of the beds in the room. "I'll go ahead and take the luggage cart with me downstairs. Is there anything that I can do for you folks while I'm here?"

"No, you've done enough. Thank you very much for your help," said Anthony as he pulled out his wallet, removing a ten-dollar bill and giving it to Travis.

"Thank you, sir. If there is anything more that we can do for you, please just give us a call and we can be right here. Enjoy your evening, and your stay with us here at Crystal Mountain."

"Thank you, have a good night," said Elizabeth as she opened the room's door, allowing Travis to push the cart out of the room and into the hallway. Shutting the door behind him, she walked back into the room as Samantha was turning the TV on in the room.

"Mom, are we going to go check out the fireworks after dinner?" asked Samantha as she sat down on the couch with the television remote in hand.

"Yes, that's the plan. Are you ready to go?" asked Elizabeth.

"Yeah, I am."

"Where'd your dad go?"

"He went to the bathroom."

"Oh. Okay. What's on TV?"

"Not sure, I just turned it on."

"Is there a guide menu?"

"Not sure, I haven't found it yet," said Samantha as she flipped channels with the remote.

The bathroom door opened to her parent's bedroom, and her dad walked out into the living room area.

"Okay, you want to use the bathroom too?" he asked Elizabeth.

"No, I'm fine. Sam, do you need to use the bathroom?"

"No, I'm ready, Mom."

"Okay, you have your key card, hon? Sam, turn the television off and let's go get some dinner."

Samantha turned the TV off in the living room, then stood up from the couch as the family left the room together. They shut the door behind them and took the elevator from the seventh floor down to the first. The elevator doors opened, and the family stepped out and examined the map of the first floor posted on the wall by the elevators.

"Okay, so that Chinese restaurant is past the lobby, around the corner, down the hallway past the gift shop and next to the pool area. Come on, you guys," said Anthony.

"I hope you don't need a reservation for dinner," said Elizabeth.

"I'm sure it'll be fine," replied Anthony as they started walking past the hallway.

Sitting in a cushioned chair in the lobby away from the front desk was a balding middle-aged man wearing faded blue jeans, a purple windbreaker. He stroked his beard stubble and adjusted his bifocals, watching Samantha and her parents walking through the lobby. After they passed, the man stood up and followed them from a distance, careful not to get too close, tracking them in between the crowd of guests.

"What beautiful decorations they have here at the resort," said Samantha.

"I love the architecture here, and the artwork they have on the walls too," said Anthony as the family turned and walked into the packed Chinese restaurant toward the hostess stand.

"Good evening. Welcome to Pek Kin Palace. How many are in your party tonight?" asked the hostess.

"Good evening, there are three of us," said Anthony.

"Table for three is about a ten-minute wait. We just need to clean off a couple tables, then we'll get you seated. It won't be long."

"No problem, thank you," said Elizabeth as the family turned around and walked over to a cushioned seating area and sat down to wait.

"So, what do you want to do tomorrow, Sam?" asked Anthony.

"Rides. Oh, breakfast at the Character Resort breakfast party first. Then rides."

"Fireworks tomorrow night, too?"

"And tonight."

"What about the water park?" asked Elizabeth.

"We can do that part of the park in the next couple of days," replied Samantha.

"Owen, party of three?" said the hostess.

"Okay, that's us," said Anthony as the family stood up and walked up to the counter.

"We're Owen, party of three," said Elizabeth.

"Great, right this way," said the hostess, grabbing three menus and leading the family into the restaurant.

After they left the front counter, the man who followed them snuck into the restaurant, unbeknownst to anyone working there. He walked through the dining area and let himself into the kitchen, where he grabbed a white apron and put it on. He blended into the large group of chefs, who were also wearing aprons in the kitchen.

Meanwhile, the hostess sat Samantha and her family at a table next to the glass wall, overlooking the pool area. The resort theme park pool experience went beyond just the water features. At the Crystal Mountain Theme Park and Resort, poolside restaurants and snack bars served refreshing drinks and snacks, ensuring families could stay fueled and hydrated throughout the day. Live music played in the courtyard area by the pool, and character meet-and-greets were happening all around the poolside area, further enhancing the festive atmosphere. Samantha looked out on the pool area through the restaurant glass windows with excitement in her eyes. While she was looking out the window, the waitress, a middle-aged woman with red hair and a bright glowing smile on her face, came to their table with glasses of water.

"Good evening you guys. Welcome to Pek Kin Palace. My name is Jennifer, and I will be your waitress for the evening," she said, setting down the glasses of water on the table and passing them out to each person. "Can I start you off with something to drink besides water?"

"I'll have an orange soda if you have it?" asked Anthony.

"We do have that."

"And I'll take cola," said Elizabeth.

"And for you, my dear?" Jennifer asked Samantha.

"Root beer for me."

"You got it. Here are our menus," said the waitress as she handed out the menus. "The specials for tonight are kung pao chicken with fried rice, chow mein with egg flower soup, and dim sum with steamed greens."

"Oh, sounds good. I may have some kung pao chicken," said Anthony.

"I'll give you folks a minute to decide and then I'll be right back with your drinks."

"Thank you, ma'am."

Jennifer turned and walked away, to speak with another table nearby before going back to get drinks for everyone. Samantha and her parents looked through the menu, then at the specials, then back at the menu again.

"Still getting sweet and sour chicken, Sam?" asked Anthony.

"Yup."

"I think I'm going to get General Tso chicken for dinner," said Elizabeth.

"Hey that sounds good. I think I'll do the kung pao chicken special myself."

"Have you folks decided on what you want for dinner tonight?" asked Jennifer as she returned with their drinks.

"Yes, I'm going to have the kung pao chicken special," said Anthony.

"Sounds good. That comes with the fried rice on the side. And for you?" she asked, looking at Elizabeth.

"I'm going to do the General Tso chicken."

"That comes with your choice of fried rice or egg flower soup."

"Egg flower soup, please."

"Good choice, and for you, honey?" She asked, looking at Samantha.

"Sweet and sour chicken, please."

"That's my favorite! It comes with fried rice; does that work okay?"

"It does."

"Okay, you've got it. I'll be right back with your food here in a bit."

The waitress turned and walked back toward the kitchen area, giving the order to the cooks in the kitchen.

"Here. Table forty-four. General Tso for the wife. Kung pao special for the husband. Make it extra spicy. And sweet and sour chicken for their daughter," said Jennifer to the balding middle-aged chef.

The chefs reviewed the orders and began making the meals for guests in the restaurant, while Samantha excitedly explained to her mom and dad how she wanted to spend her week in the park, starting with the fireworks show this evening. When the chefs finished cooking their dishes, the balding middle-aged chef stepped aside for a moment, retrieving a small stainless-steel vial from his pocket. Twisting it open, he poured a white powder over the top of the sweet and sour chicken. He put the vial back into his pocket and set the three plates down on the serving counter as he rang the bell. Afterwards, he turned around and walked away from the counter, back into the kitchen and disappeared from the front. Jennifer came back and picked up the dishes on her serving tray, completely unaware that the chicken had been poisoned.

She took the food over to Samantha's table and served everyone their dish. The family began eating and enjoying their meal while watching kids and families play in the pool under the lights. Samantha ate everything on her plate, followed by Anthony, who was sweating from eating the kung pao chicken with extra spice. Elizabeth was the last to finish her meal, cleaning her plate. A short time later, Jennifer came back over to the table.

"Okay, you guys, would you be interested in some dessert this evening?"

"Oh no, I'm full," said Elizabeth.

"So am I, Sam. What about you?"

"No, nothing for me either," she said, taking a sip of her root beer.

"We need to get going to get a good spot for the fireworks this evening," said Elizabeth.

"Oh yes! That show starts in about fifteen minutes."

"Fifteen minutes? I thought the show was at 8:00 PM?"

"Oh no, not tonight. The show is at 7:00 PM."

"Can you charge the meal to our room?"

"Sure, what's your room number?"

"Room 714."

"Okay, room 714. Got it. Would you like to add a tip?"

"Sure, fifteen dollars, please."

"Thank you for that."

"What's the quickest way to the fireworks show?" asked Anthony.

"If you go past the pool outside, head down the walkway. You're going to see a lot of folks going there, anyway. Once you pass the pool, you'll see a crowd walking towards the south end of the park, where the bay is. Just keep following them and you'll be there in about ten minutes."

"We've gotta get going then. Thank you for dinner this evening, and thanks for the directions, too."

"No problem, enjoy the show and come on back for dinner again!" said Jennifer.

Samantha and her parents stood up and left the restaurant. They walked past the pool and out into the crowd of people. Anthony and her mom leading the way to the fireworks display.

And then she felt it. Slight dizziness and nausea.

"Hey Mom, I'm not feeling too good?" said Samantha, through the crowd to her mom.

"What, oh, this way, honey. Follow me," said Elizabeth, who hadn't heard Samantha clearly because of the noise and chatter from the surrounding crowd.

"Mom," said Samantha as she started to lag a little bit behind them, watching her parents get further into the crowd, but still able to see them. Her head started to get numb, and she began to feel sleepy.

"I really don't feel good," she mumbled.

"Honey, try to keep up," said Elizabeth as she turned around and saw Samantha still following them. She turned around, her and Anthony trying to find a clear path through the already large forming crowd around them.

Samantha did her best to keep up, but she started to get further and further away from her parents. Her eyes started to glaze over, and her vision blurred. She slowed down considerably now when someone grabbed her by the hand and walked her away. Her knees began to give out when she felt herself slinking down to the pavement. Samantha then felt herself get picked up and carried, assuming that it was her father now carrying her the rest of the way to the fireworks display.

Slowly, she slipped into a deep sleep as the balding man in the purple windbreaker carried her towards the entrance of the park and out into the parking lot.

Chapter 6: Miami, Florida to Tallahassee, Florida on Interstate 95

Samantha started to wake up. She lay on her side on a hard cold floor; her feet and arms bound in place. The floor vibrated slightly as she rolled onto her back and sat up to look around. Both her parents were gone, and she could tell that she was no longer in the park, but in the back of an old van as it drove down the road. It was dark out. The only light in the van came from the illuminated instruments on the dashboard and the passing headlights of motor vehicles going the opposite direction that temporarily lit up the inside of the van. Two men sat in the two seats in front of her, staring straight ahead. The more she started to regain consciousness, the more she was able to hear that they were talking among themselves while they drove her down the road.

"How long of a drive you think it will be?" asked the passenger.

"Los Angeles is quite a long way from Miami, Carl," said the driver.

"Over 2700 miles of driving I-10 across the country, Bo. Should take us a solid two to three days driving out there, I'd imagine," said Carl.

"We got something to snack on? I'm hungry."

The passenger reached back, grabbing a plastic grocery bag from behind the center console.

"Beef stick?" asked Carl.

"No, I'm thinking of something sweet."

"Hostess cupcakes?"

"Yeah, sure."

Carl handed a package of cupcakes to the driver.

"Jesus Christ, 2700 miles. Sometimes I tell myself I could just stay at home, not bother with this shit anymore and scam old women out of their life savings off the internet. Fuckin Medicare is there for them anyway, ya know?" said Bo as he turned to look for a moment at Carl.

"Even that doesn't pay nearly as well as teenage girls, Bo. You know that."

"Hey, listen. I was thinking along the way, why don't we pull over somewhere off in the desert and see what she has to offer?"

"No. We aren't bangin a teenager, Bo, especially one that still has her virginity. Virgins bring in almost double the price that a non-virgin would bring in. I swear to God, if I see your dick out of your pants, I'll kill you myself. Don't cost me money, Bo."

"Alright, Jesus Carl. I'm not saying bang her, I'm just saying see what she has, ya know?"

"I suggest you don't even bother and just keep your focus on the money."

"Alright, alright. So how much do you think we could get for this one?"

"Sex trade? Good money. Early teens. Just started developing. I'd imagine she doesn't even have to shave herself either. Those fuckers will pay good money. Especially when they find out she's a virgin."

"How do you know she's a virgin, Carl?"

"I think it's a safe assumption. That's how we're going to advertise her anyway. You just go with what I say and do not touch this one."

"Are we still going to stop in Sonora at the chicken farm?" asked Bo.

"We are, yes. We might be picking up another girl there to take with us. Mr. Harkin called me the other day and told me that one of the families that he bought to work the farm had a nice ripe sixteen-year-old. Big tits at sixteen already, too. The lucky bastard will probably make a decent chunk of change keeping her out of the chicken farm and putting her up for auction."

"Could we check her out too when we pick her up?"

"We aren't checking any one of them out, other than to figure out a price to mark their arms with."

"How will you know what they are worth if you don't give them a try?"

"God damn it, Bo. I told you, fuck this up for us and I'm going to kill you. Make good choices."

"Ah, shit," said Bo.

"What is it now?"

"She's awake in the back."

Carl glanced over his shoulder, seeing that Samantha was awake and looking forward, trying to figure out what was going on. Carl unbuckled himself from his seat and moved past the center floor console between the seats and crawled into the back, sitting on the floor next to Samantha.

"Hey, how are you? Do you remember me?" asked Carl.

Samantha didn't respond to his question.

"Remember, I was at the airport in Chicago. Then on the plane to Miami, Carl. My name is Carl."

"Where am I?" asked a groggy Samantha.

"Well, right now you're in the back of my van, you see. We just passed Naples, Florida. On our way to Interstate ten."

"Where are we going?" Asked Samantha, as she rubbed her eyes with her thumbs, as her arms were tied together, but in front of her.

"Well. Samantha, that's going to be a surprise. We're going to go and pick up a friend tomorrow. Someone we're going to introduce you to, and then we're taking you to California."

"California? Why?"

"Well. You'll find out when we get there," said Carl, with a smile on his face. "Until then though, would you like something to eat? We got meat sticks. Chips. You thirsty?"

"No."

"Oh, come on now, Samantha. I know that after you wake up from Rohypnol you get thirsty. Bo, give me a bottle of water."

The driver reached into another bag in the center floor console and grabbed a water bottle, reaching behind and handing it to Carl.

"Here, have some water," said Carl, opening the bottle and handing it to her.

Samantha took the bottle, took a drink of the water and then lowered her chin onto her chest.

"Are you feeling sick? Dizzy still? Tired?"

"Tired. A little sick."

"Symptoms are mild. They will be gone in no time. For now, why don't you get some rest and just relax for a bit? Tomorrow morning when you're feeling better then maybe we can talk a little more about where you're going."

Carl grabbed the bottle of water from Samantha, forcing her to lie back down on the floor of the van. He grabbed a pillow from the back of the van, positioning it under her head, and then grabbed a blanket and, in the same manner, covered her body as she slowly drifted off into a deep sleep.

*　　　*　　　*　　　*

Samantha started to wake up in the back of the van again. This time the van was filled with light, and it had stopped moving. She sat in the back and looked around. The effects of the Rohypnol had worn off, and Samantha was much more aware of what was happening now. She had been kidnapped. She had no idea where she was other than in the back of a van on the outskirts of a parking lot. Her hands were bound in front of her, and her feet were still tied together, too. She managed to get up to her knees, then stood up using the side of the van to help push herself up. She tried opening the doors in the back of the van, but the doors were locked. The locking and unlocking mechanisms had been altered in such a way that the doors could only be opened from the outside.

She tried the doors up in front of the van but found that these doors too were locked. The windows in the front of the van were heavily tinted with the exception of the windshield, which also had a thick strip of window tinting at the very top of the windshield, like a visor. She looked out the window and saw vehicles parked in the distance. A small café that served breakfast, lunch, and dinner stood in front of her. She banged on the side of the van and yelled as loud as she could, but no one nearby heard her.

She looked around the front of the van for a tool or device to help cut herself free. Sitting in the passenger seat, she opened the glove box and rummaged through it. Looking towards the back of the glove box, she found a flathead screwdriver that she grabbed from the box. Taking it in both hands, she leaned down and used the tool to cut into the side of the duct tape around her ankles. It took a while, but eventually she was able to cut into the duct tape enough so that she could force her feet out and tear through the weakened tape, freeing her legs.

Samantha took the screwdriver and did her best to weaken the duct tape around her wrists. It took nearly twice as long to break through the duct tape tying her wrists together, but eventually she was able to break through the tape, and now her arms were free. At that moment though, two men walked out of the diner. One carried a plastic bag in hand as they walked towards the van.

Samantha quickly got out of the passenger seat, into the back of the van. She tried using the screwdriver to break through the glass in the back doors of the van, but no matter how hard she hit the glass, the screwdriver simply bounced off it. It wasn't regular glass. She positioned herself next to the passenger seat. Ready to jump out the moment the door was opened. Of the two men, one approached the passenger door. She could hear the door unlock and then the handle being pulled, and then the door was opened.

Samantha leaped out of the van, lunging at the man with the screwdriver. The man quickly sidestepped her, grabbing her at the same time. She dropped the screwdriver on the ground as she struggled in his arms to break free.

"Well, how the fuck did you get loose so fast? We were only in the café for forty-five minutes," said Carl.

Bo got into the driver's side and shut the door behind him. Samantha screamed, hoping that someone would hear her fight for freedom and help, but no one did. When Carl shoved her back into the van, Bo grabbed a handful of her hair on the back of her head and pulled her in, forcing her face down against the van's floor.

"After we got you breakfast, no less, you try to pull a stunt like that. You seriously could have hurt me with that screwdriver. I thought we were better friends than that, Sam," said Carl as he climbed into the van and shut the door behind him as Bo started the van, and the doors automatically locked.

"Now, I'll make a deal with you. You get in the back of the van. I'll give you your breakfast. You sit back there, and you don't do anything crazy. Like trying to jab a fuckin screwdriver into my face, and we won't have any problems. Got it?"

"Okay," Samantha replied, her face still pressed into the floor of the passenger side of the van.

"Did you take anything else you shouldn't have?" said Carl, feeling her pant pockets and pant waistband down.

"No, I didn't."

"You're goddamn right you didn't. Now get the fuck back there!" he yelled as Bo picked her up and then Carl shoved her into the back of the van. Samantha lost her balance and fell into the back of the van.

"Here's your breakfast," said Carl, tossing the plastic bag with a takeout box in it. He opened the center floor console of the van and grabbed a water bottle from it.

"Here's some water for you too. Maybe you'll remember how nice I've been to you this whole time the next time you get the urge to try to kill me, you stupid little bitch," said Carl as he tossed the water bottle back at her.

Bo started the van, and within a few minutes, they were headed to the freeway entrance to Interstate 10. Samantha took the takeout box, opening it to reveal a piece of toast and some leftover scrambled eggs and hashbrowns. She searched through the bag, looking for a fork, but there was none. Using her hands, she picked up what she could and ate.

"I think we are going to connect with Interstate seventy-five here soon, then that'll take us up to Interstate ten. From there we'll head east to Texas," said Carl, looking at the GPS map on his phone.

"How long until we're in Texas?" asked Bo.

"Fifteen hundred miles. A solid day's drive from Tampa."

"Holy shit, man. We need to find girls closer to California. How long you want me to drive?"

"You can drive eight hours. I'll take the next eight. We'll just take it in eight-hour shifts until we get to Sonora and then eventually Los Angeles."

"Great. Well, you'd better get some rest. I'll wake you up here at six this evening," said Bo.

"Alright, you know where you're going?"

"Yeah, north to Interstate 75, north to Interstate 10, then west to Texas. Got it."

"Alright," said Carl, as he turned around in his seat, propping his head up against the window. He shut his eyes, and a short time later, he drifted off to sleep.

"So, what grade are you in, kid?"

"I just graduated from the sixth grade a couple of months ago."

"No shit. You're a seventh grader? You're developing at a young age."

Samantha didn't say anything to the man.

"It's okay; you can talk to me. I won't bite. So, where are you from?"

"Park Forest."

"Park Forest? Where the fuck is that?"

"Chicago."

"No shit. I had a cousin who lived in Chicago for a little bit. Never went and visited him. I'm Bo, by the way."

Samantha didn't answer him.

"I said my name is Bo. What's your name?"

"Samantha."

"Samantha? That's a really pretty name. You have any brothers or sisters?"

"No."

"Friends?"

"From school."

"Nice. I had friends in school before I joined a gang; then I had some new friends. Haven't seen them in quite a while though. It was just a local gang. I dropped out of school for them, and then they just stopped hanging out, so fuck 'em right?"

"I guess."

"Both your parents married or not?"

"Yeah."

"Nice. I never really met my dad. He was out of the picture when my mom was pregnant with me. Mom worked most of the time, two jobs. I was on my own a lot while I was growing up. Always getting in trouble as a kid. My last teacher in high school before I dropped out called me a shit for brains loser. Can you believe that?

Coming from a teacher? Shit, I guess he was right though. Well, I guess it's all in how you look at it. I'm making a good living doing what I'm doing."

"What are you doing?"

"Trafficking. Sex trade. All that shit. I started out with labor trafficking. Transporting kids from the border to farms and shit around Texas and Louisiana. But then I found out there's a lot more money moving kids for sex. And along the way, maybe having a bit of fun myself too. But the money trading one kid for sex is three times as better than taking a van of Mexican kids to the farms and selling them there, ya know?"

"Please take me back to my mom and dad," said Samantha.

"No can do, honey. You know how much you're worth? Girl your age, developed the way you are? Bare minimum, fifty grand. And I bet we can doll you up and get even more. Carl here and I, when he told me all about you when he saw you at the theme park, he told me that we had a real diamond in the rough. And I gotta say I would agree with him. I wouldn't mind seeing more of you too."

"Please let me go."

"Sorry honey. Not going to let fifty grand just walk away like that. I'm sure you'll be bought by someone who will take good care of you."

*   *   *   *

"So, tell me, when was the last time you saw your daughter?" asked the police detective who was questioning Anthony and Elizabeth in their room at the resort.

"We left dinner. We were going to go see the fireworks for the night. It was crowded, and we were making our way through the crowd. It was dusk too, not completely dark," said a distraught Anthony.

"She had complained about a stomachache, but we had just had some Chinese food at the park here, and sometimes her stomach hurts after eating Chinese," said Elizabeth, equally distraught.

"So, you were making your way through the crowd, and then what happened?"

"I swear, she was right behind me. We finally found a spot where we could stand and watch the fireworks. I turned around, and she wasn't there."

The detective leaned over to another detective, who was standing beside him, whispering in his ear.

"Go to the park security office, see if they have security video of the park from last night around 8:30 PM."

The second detective left the room to go speak with the security office of the park.

"Now, is it possible that she may have just got lost in the park somewhere?"

"No, I don't think so. We think she was kidnapped. Security helped us last night to try to find her. The other Miami officers who came out and tried to help us find her. We've been walking through the park all night and can't find her anywhere."

"Okay, so let me make sure I understand right. Her name is Samantha Owens. She is twelve years old, yes?"

"That's right, sir," said Anthony.

"Stands about four feet, eleven inches. One hundred and five pounds. Dark brown hair that hangs down past her shoulders at about the midway point in her back?"

"Yes, sir. She just had a birthday last month on the eighteenth."

"So, she just turned twelve not that long ago. You folks know anyone down here?"

"No, we don't."

"You say you think she was kidnapped. What makes you think that?"

"If she were still here, my wife and I would have found her. We've looked everywhere here in the park. All night."

"And what was she wearing?"

"Blue jeans. Brown T-shirt. White tennis shoes."

"Does she wear her hair in a certain way?"

"She may tie it in a ponytail, or pigtails, but no, her hair is just straight back."

The detective's phone rang in his shirt breast pocket. He apologized and excused himself for a moment, answering the phone.

"Hello?"

Anthony and Elizabeth watched as the detective answered the phone with short responses such as "okay" and finished with an "I'll be right there." The officer hung up the phone and turned around to speak with Samantha's parents.

"Are you folks going to be here for a bit longer?" he asked.

"Yes, sir. We are," said Anthony.

"Stay here. I'll be right back," he said as he turned and walked out of the room.

The detective walked out of the hotel resort and across the front driveway of the hotel, over to the security office. When he approached the door of the office, he knocked, and the second detective opened the door, allowing him access to the security office. Inside, two of the resort's security guards were reviewing video from the night before. Multiple views of security surveillance in the parks interior and exterior were viewed in a dimly lit monitor room.

"Okay, what did you find?" asked the first detective as he approached the monitors where security was viewing video.

"Something interesting, Nate. Check this out," said the other detective.

One of the security officers reached over, pushing play on the computer screen. Digital video began to play on the main walkway, leading to the lagoon area. The last place that Samantha was seen by her parents when she was complaining of stomach pains. The men watched as they could see Anthony and Elizabeth walking through a large crowd, followed by their daughter, who was lagging behind them. They were able to observe on video a middle-aged man, balding. With some beard stubble on his face, that looked as if he had shaved yesterday morning. He wore bifocals, a purple windbreaker jacket and old faded blue jeans. The man approached the left side of Samantha, grabbed her hand and walked her away from her parents through the crowd.

"It looks as if she was kidnapped, Nate," said the second detective.

"Certainly, looks to me like we have a child abduction crime. Is there any other video of them?" asked Nate.

"There is. The park entrance," said the security guard. With a couple of clicks of the mouse, he pulled up video of the park entrance on the computer. They watched as the man carried Samantha in his arms out of the park.

"Where'd they go?" asked Nate.

"Lot C, but far and away in the lot," said one of the security guards, who switched videos on the computer to lot C's parking.

"This is the best you have from here?" asked Nate.

"As good as it gets. The other camera down at that end is waiting for some parts to come in from China to fix it and get it working again."

"Of course. All I can see are small pixel dots. Are we sure that's them?"

"I'm guessing so. It's the same direction that the man was walking when he went out of frame in the previous video."

The man approached a large white vehicle, opened the door and made some unclear motions on the blurred video before shutting the door. Afterwards, he got inside the front passenger door, and the white vehicle took off, out of the lot.

"And that's it, isn't it?" asked Nate.

"Sure as hell is," said the second detective.

"No video of the exit?"

"None."

"Fuck. Well, what do you think that vehicle was?"

"Van? SUV? Hell, maybe a truck with a canopy on the back. Who knows? The video is too grainy to see exactly what kind of vehicle it is. It's not a truck. Not a car."

"Okay. So, it's safe to assume that the girl is kidnapped. Tossed into the back of a white, larger-sized vehicle. Taken God knows where at this point," said the second detective.

"Didn't the family say that they had dinner at the Chinese restaurant here at the resort?" asked Nate.

The second detective opened his notepad, flipping through his notes and reading them.

"Uhhh, yeah. They mentioned that they checked in. The bellhop escorted them to their room with their luggage. Then, when they were unpacked, they came down to the lobby, walked over to the Chinese restaurant called Pek Kin Palace here in the hotel. Had dinner. Then they were on their way to the lagoon to see the fireworks, and that's when they noticed that she was lost."

"Pek Kin, that's the place next to the pool downstairs, yeah?" asked the first detective.

"Yes, it's down near the lobby of the resort hotel. Windows overlooking the pool area," said one of the security guards in reply.

"You've got cameras down by the restaurant?" asked the first detective.

"We have cameras in the lobby and the hallway leading down to that restaurant. Then cameras on the pool, but that is it."

"You don't have cameras in the restaurant?" asked the first detective.

"We do. We just don't control them here. They're in the manager's office of the restaurant. You'd have to go talk to him."

"What's his name?"

"Zhang. Jiang Zhang. He's been a manager at the restaurant for the last five years now. Graduated from a culinary school in San Diego, and instead of moving back to Nanjing over in China, he decided to stay here and take the head manager's position of the restaurant. Done a pretty good job in our opinion too. He will know what cameras they have there and what they can see."

"Is he here today?"

"Yeah, he's here all the time. He knows his restaurant inside and out."

"Alright. Let's go talk to Zhang then," said the first detective, as he turned and walked out of the security office.

The second detective followed close behind. They were silent as they walked through a crowd of people moving to and from rides, concession stands, and gift shops. After making their way through the crowd, they came across the resort hotel pool area, where they saw the windows of the restaurant on the opposite side of the pool. The two detectives walked around the pool and into the resort hotel lobby before turning down a long hallway to the Pek Kin Palace, where a hostess greeted them.

"Good morning, gentlemen. Would you like a table for two for breakfast?" asked the hostess at the front desk.

"No, ma'am. My name is detective Nate Gardner," said the first detective, showing his police department identification card. "This is detective Mike Crews. We need to speak with Jiang Zhang."

"Of course. Hold on one minute and let me go get him."

The hostess turned around, left the front desk as both the detectives stood and waited for her to return. Moments later, the hostess returned along with a Chinese man, who was short in stature and walking quickly behind her towards the front.

"Gentlemen. I am Jiang Zhang. Cynthia said that you would like to speak with me?" asked Jiang, the manager of the restaurant.

"Yes, sir. My name is Detective Gardner; this is Detective Crews. We would like to ask you about last night."

"Last night?"

"Here, in your restaurant. Do you happen to have security video of your restaurant?"

"Of course. Please gentlemen, follow me to my office," said Zhang as he turned and walked back to his office at the back of the restaurant.

The detectives followed him to the back office, where Jiang opened the office door, revealing a small janitor closet that had been converted into an office. A desk rested against the side wall with a computer monitor sitting on top of the desk. A five-level bookshelf against one of the walls, and the third wall had a five-shelf filing cabinet.

"I'm sorry, gentlemen, for the lack of space. Now, you said you need to see security monitors?" asked Jiang.

"Yes, that's right. Security video from last night of the restaurant?" asked Detective Gardner.

"What time, gentlemen?"

"Around 6:30 PM."

Jiang sat down at his desk, turning his computer on. When the monitor started up, he opened the security video system on his computer and reviewed the archived video of the lobby.

"Okay, what are we looking for, gentlemen?" asked Jiang.

"A family of three. Dad. Mom. Young daughter," said detective Gardner.

They fast-forwarded through the video for about half an hour. Watching crowds of customers walk through the lobby until they saw Anthony, Elizabeth, and Samantha come into the restaurant.

"There!" yelled Detective Crews.

Detective Gardner looked through his notes in his notebook, reviewing the time that Anthony had told him that they had gone to the restaurant for dinner last night.

"That's them. A little after 7:00 PM, just like the father said," said Detective Gardner. "Can we see where they went in the restaurant?"

"Wait! Look," said detective Crews, pointing at the screen.

The two detectives watched the same man who had carried Samantha out of the park walk in behind the family and into the restaurant.

"Can you follow that man, Jiang?"

The restaurant manager switched the camera to the main seating area for guests that overlooked the whole dining room area, where they saw the man walk into the room. Walking across the screen, he proceeded to go into the kitchen area.

"Did he walk into the kitchen?" asked Detective Gardner.

"That is our kitchen. Let me see if I can pull the camera in the kitchen up."

Jiang switched the camera and pulled up a camera that covered the cooking area where the chefs were working.

"No one noticed this guy in the kitchen?" asked Detective Gardner.

"It was a busy night. We have some new chefs, and I wasn't here last night. It was my day off."

"But no one noticed him?"

"It appears not."

"What is he doing now?" asked Detective Crews.

The three men watched as the man reached around the corner of the doors in the kitchen, grabbed an apron and put it on. He then moved over towards the wok range and worked a couple of the woks by the stove. Then he walked out of the kitchen for a moment, looked around the dining area, walked back into the kitchen, and hung out around the serving counter. The waitress handed him an order slip for Samantha's table after he saw her take their order. The waitress turned around and walked back into the dining room, while he took the slip and handed it to one of the chefs in the kitchen.

They then watched as the food was prepped and set on the serving table, where the man was clearly seen reaching into his pocket and taking something out. They witnessed him pour a small vial of something onto the food on one of the plates. He then placed the plates on the counter, left the tag next to the plates and rang the bell. Soon, the waitress served the food to the family. The man took off his apron, hung it back up on a hook behind the door, and exited the kitchen, walking out of the restaurant.

"Goddamn it, where did he go?" asked Detective Crews.

"I don't know; I just have access to the cameras here in the restaurant," said Jiang.

"I want to watch when the family leaves the dining room."

Jiang fast-forwarded the recorded video as it played through the family eating at the table by the windows, overlooking the pool area. It then showed the family getting up and leaving the restaurant.

"Who was the waitress that the man talked to?" asked Detective Gardner.

"Her name is Kaitlynn," said Jiang.

"Is she here?"

"She will be here in the next ten minutes," Jiang replied as he looked at the watch on his wrist.

"I want to know what he was talking to her about. Can you call her in early?"

"Sure, I can see where she's at."

Jiang picked up the phone on his desk. Flipping through the contacts list, he found the phone number for Kaitlynn and called her. The phone rang a couple times and was then answered by the waitress.

"Kaitlynn, it's Jiang. Listen, when will you be here for your shift this morning?" he asked. "Oh, you are walking in right now. Come to my office. No, you are not in trouble. There are a couple of detectives here, and they want to ask you a couple of questions. Okay, see you in a minute."

Jiang hung up the phone, turned and looked at the detectives.

"She is just walking in through the lobby right now. She will be on her way. Can I ask what this is all about?"

"Not sure we can answer that just yet, but our best guess is that we are dealing with a child kidnapping."

"Oh, dear. That is not good."

"No, it's not."

The office door opened, and in walked the waitress from last night, who had served Anthony, Elizabeth, and Samantha's table.

"Hi, are you Kaitlynn?" asked Detective Gardner.

"Yeah, is something wrong?" she asked.

"There is, but you're not in trouble. We just need to ask you a few questions. You worked last night, did you not?"

"Yes, I did."

"Do you recall serving the family of three by the window? Man, woman, and young girl."

"Which table?"

"Can you show her the table and family, Jiang?"

Jiang rewound the video on the monitor and showed the family to the waitress.

"Oh, yes. I do remember them. I served them," said Kaitlynn, looking at the computer monitor.

"There was a man in the kitchen who you had handed the order slip to after taking their order."

"Yes, one of the chefs. I think he was new. I know we had a couple of new chefs start working in the kitchen for us last night. I just assumed he was one of the new ones."

"Do you recall what he said to you?"

"Yeah, he asked me what the slip was for. So, I pointed to the family by the window at table twenty-seven."

"Did he ask or say anything else?"

"Yeah, he asked which dish was for which family member. So, I told him, the dad ordered the kung pao chicken special that comes with a side of fried rice. The woman ordered General Tso's chicken with a side of egg flower soup. And the young girl ordered the sweet and sour chicken with fried rice."

"So that's how he knew which dish was the girls'," said Detective Crews.

"Did he say anything else to you?" asked Detective Gardner.

"No, he just took the order, asked the questions, thanked me and went back into the kitchen from the serving counter."

"So, he spiked the food with something. Caused the girl to get sick, then pass out, which made it easier for him to come by and snag her up and carry her right out of the park."

"Classic kidnapping, Nate."

The detectives took down the names and phone numbers of the restaurant manager and the waitress, then left the restaurant. They went upstairs to Anthony and Elizabeth's room on the seventh floor, where they shared the bad news with them about what they had found out and seen from the video.

Anthony and Elizabeth wept. Coming to the realization that there was a chance that Samantha was gone forever, and there was nothing they could do about it.

Chapter 7: Mobile, Alabama

The old fortified white van drove down Interstate 10 along the north panhandle region of Florida. One man sat in the passenger seat, sleeping. His head was propped up against the passenger-side window. The driver, grabbing a bottle of soda from the cup holder, opened the bottle and took a drink. Twisting the bottle back onto the lid, he set it back in the cupholder, yawned, and continued driving as the wipers on the windshield swished back and forth, wiping rainwater from the windshield.

In the back of the van, Samantha Owens propped her back up against the van's side paneling. She felt every bump on the road as they drove along the interstate. She had spent most of the morning crying in the back of the van. Of the small amount of food that the kidnappers had given her, she barely ate any. Panic engulfed her emotions, and she feared what would become of her the further she was driven away from her parents in Florida.

"Listen. You really have got nothing to worry about. Chances are good that you're going to get to stay locally in California. I'll bet an American buys you. Maybe one of the Chinese businessmen that usually go to these auctions, but usually those guys are American too," said Bo from the driver's seat, watching Samantha in the rear-view mirror.

"I need to use the bathroom," said Samantha.

"No problem. You know what, this piece of shit has been sleeping for long enough anyway. He needs to take his turn driving. Carl!" yelled Bo from the driver's seat, using his hand to nudge Carl awake.

Carl woke up in the passenger seat. He rubbed his eyes with both his hands as he leaned back up in his seat and looked out the front window.

"What? What's the problem?" he asked.

"Girl needs to use the bathroom," said Bo.

"Great, goddamn it. Why did you wake me up for that? Just take her to an outhouse at a gas station along the way," said Carl as he slouched in his seat and started going back to sleep.

"No, man, I've been driving all night and into the morning. You take over for a bit. I need some rest too," said Bo.

"Ahh shit," said Carl, as he sat back up again.

"Which exit should we take?" asked Bo.

"I don't give a shit. Whichever one has a bathroom outside the station. She doesn't need her mouthing off to someone about her situation."

"There. How about the Quincy rest area?" Said Bo.

"Sure. If they have got a family bathroom, take her in there," said Carl.

The van pulled off the highway exit and into the rest area. There were only a couple of other vehicles present along with a couple of truckers on the trucker side of the rest stop. One of the older couples who had stopped walked out of the family bathroom, which was a single-room bathroom for families to use if one member needed assistance using the restroom apart from the public stalls. The old man helped walk his frail wife out by the arm, back to their vehicle in the lot where he helped her into the car. Both Bo and Carl watched as the old man got into the car after helping his wife in and watched as they drove away, leaving only one other car behind.

"Probably going to be as clear as it ever will be. Let's go. Sam, I swear to God if you scream or so much as say a word, I'll fuckin kill you. You understand me? Don't be stupid," said Carl.

Samantha nodded.

"You go into the stall with her. Make sure she doesn't do something stupid," said Carl, talking to Bo.

"Yeah, sure. I got this," said Bo as he opened the door.

Carl opened his door, and the two men got out. Carl leaned back inside and motioned for Samantha to come out the passenger side door with him, which she did. When she was out of the van, Carl took her by the arm and walked her to the family restroom. Bo walked ahead of them, and he opened the door to the large family-sized bathroom. Carl shoved her into the room, with Bo following closely behind. He shut the door on the two and stood guard as Bo locked the door from the inside.

"Okay, go," said Bo, standing there, watching her.

"I can't go if you're watching me."

The kidnapper turned his back to her as she went to use the toilet. Out of the corner of his eye, he watched her in the mirror without her knowing it.

"You know, I had a daughter once," said Bo.

Samantha didn't respond to him, but sat on the toilet, taking care of her business.

"I was even married at one time too. A couple years after being together, we had a daughter together. It was so perfect. Absolutely perfect. I loved getting up at night. One, two in the morning. Walking into her bedroom when she was crying. Picking her up and rocking her to sleep. I remember the early years of her life. Then her toddler years, too. A lot of parents hated it when their kids would throw fits in the store when they didn't get the toy they wanted, or the candy bar. But I didn't mind it. It was parenthood, ya know? It made me feel alive and important. And then it happened. When she was five. My wife came home early from shopping for groceries at the store that afternoon. She came upstairs to our bedroom. Looking for me. Found me in the shower with our daughter. That bitch. She wouldn't believe me when I told her I was showering at the same time as our daughter and helping her clean up. She returned from playing in the rain covered in mud and grass clippings. So, I took her into the shower and figured that I could shower too. I wasn't touching her out of pleasure; I was touching her to help clean her body. Just like she was touching me to help me clean. There's nothing wrong with that, right?"

Samantha stood up off the toilet, pulling her pants back up to her waist and buttoning them. She flushed the toilet, then quietly walked over to the sink to wash her hands.

"No, there's nothing wrong with it. I got no pleasure from showering with her. But my wife didn't believe me. She called the police. They came. I got arrested. CPS came and took the child. I don't think the dumb bitch thought about that part either, ya know? She divorced me, and I heard months later she got custody of our daughter back. She's living in Houston now. Near her parents. Of course, my ass got in trouble for it all because I'm a man, and that's how it works in this fucking country. Found guilty on some bullshit charge that I had sexually molested my own daughter. Can you believe that shit? Now I'm on a sex registry and have been for a number of years. It's not my fault. You understand, right? What if your dad showered with you? Not now. I mean when you were five years old. That would be okay, right?" asked Bo.

Samantha finished washing her hands. She dried them with a paper towel and tossed the towel in the trash.

"All ready?" Asked Bo.

Samantha didn't respond.

"Yeah, you're all ready to go," said Bo, but before he opened the door to the family bathroom, he pinned Samantha up against the wall, pushing his hands into her shoulders.

"It's okay, right? There was nothing wrong with doing that, right?" he asked, bringing his face close to hers.

"I guess," replied Samantha, just wanting to be out of the situation and willing to say anything to make him stop pushing her up against the wall the way he was. She felt powerless, unable to fight back even if she wanted to.

"Good. Good girl. Thank you for seeing things my way. It's reassuring to me. I would never fuck my own daughter. That's disgusting," he said, releasing her from the wall.

Bo opened the door, and the moment the door was opened just a crack, she wedged her way out the door. Only to be met by Carl, who was standing there by the door on the other side.

"Jesus Christ, what took so long?" he asked them.

"Nothing, she was just washing her hands," said Bo.

"Good. Glad to hear that hygiene is something that you practice. Good hygiene will help to fetch a good price too. Come on," said Carl, as he grabbed her by the arm and walked her back to the van. He opened the passenger door, forcing Samantha into the back of the van. He shut the passenger door behind her, then turned to look at Bo.

"Got the keys?"

Bo reached into his pocket and pulled them out, handing him the keys. Carl took them, walked around to the other side and let himself in on the driver's side while Bo got into the passenger side of the van.

"Get me something to drink from the cooler," said Carl as he shut the driver's side door, buckling himself in.

Bo reached into the cooler in the front and pulled out a bottle of soda. Handing it to Carl, he set it down in the cup holder on the side of the door. Carl put the keys in the ignition, started the van, and got back onto the freeway.

"You guys talk while in the bathroom?" asked Carl as he picked the van up to speed on the interstate.

"No. Didn't talk at all," replied Bo.

"Good."

"How far away is Mobile, Bo?"

"Three more hours. Couple hundred miles up the road."

"Then from there how much further to Sonora in Texas?"

"Fuck, that's about half a day's drive. Nonstop. We still have a way to go to the chicken farm."

"You want to call Mr. Harkin and see if he still wants to sell that sixteen-year-old Mexican bitch?" asked Carl.

"I'm sure he does, but yeah, I can call," replied Bo, reaching into his pocket and pulling out his cell phone.

Samantha watched as he turned his phone on, dialed a phone number, and brought the phone up to the side of his head.

"Mr. Harkin," said Bo into the receiver of his phone.

The conversation went silent for a moment before he started speaking again.

"We're at least a couple more hours east of Mobile, Alabama, sir." Again, a period of silence, as Bo was listening to Mr. Harkin over the phone.

"I know, sir. We can have them there on Saturday. That's no issue. And we're still picking up the one from your farm in Sonora, sir."

There was silence for a moment as Samantha faintly heard a voice talking on the other end of the phone receiver.

"Yes, sir. We can be there tomorrow, no problem. Carl and I are taking turns driving so we can be on the road the whole time."

There was another pause.

"Oh, she's beautiful, Mr. Harkin. Twelve years old. Just starting to develop curves in all the right places. Dark brown hair that goes about halfway down her back."

Bo was stopped in mid conversation, as Samantha heard the man talking on the phone to Bo.

"Yes, sir. No scars or defects of any kind, sir," said Bo.

"Yes, sir. Carl thinks that she could go for at least $50,000 in auction. At this age and developing the way she is, she would make someone a happy man. Or woman. We don't judge unless it's not American dollars."

Bo nodded as he listened. "Alright, sir. We will see you here tonight No problem," he said, hanging up the phone and setting it on the dash.

"You really think we can get there by tonight?" asked Carl.

"If we go nonstop and do what we're doing, we should make it just fine," said Bo.

"I'm thirsty," said Samantha.

"Jesus Christ, if we didn't have to keep you healthy for auction this weekend, I'd say I don't care," said Bo, reaching into the cooler and pulling out a small bottle of water.

"Here," he said, tossing the bottle at Samantha, hitting her in the leg.

She grabbed the small bottle, opened it and drank the contents practically in one gulp.

"Alright, I'll drive us to Houston, then you will take us the rest of the way to Sonora."

"I can do that."

"Alright then, get some rest, alright?"

"You gonna be okay if I do?"

"I'll be fine. Get some rest."

Bo leaned the seat back a little and slowly drifted off to sleep.

It was silent in the van now aside from the hum of the tires on the road and the adjacent traffic.

"You want to listen to some music?" asked Carl.

Samantha didn't acknowledge him. She sat quietly with her back propped against the side of the van. Her knees were tucked into her chest as she wrapped her arms around them.

"I like classical music, to tell you the truth. Beethoven. Mozart. Even a little Bach goes a long way, you know?" said Carl as he fidgeted with the radio.

"I have a CD already in there, just need to hit play," he said as he continued to fumble with the faceplate of the radio.

Once he figured it out, the speakers began playing Fur Elise, by Beethoven. A simple piano tune, both charming and melancholic.

"Oh, Beethoven. One of my favorites. Have you heard of him?" Carl asked as he looked in the rear-view mirror, watching Samantha.

But she didn't acknowledge him or even look up to make eye contact with him.

"Look, I want to try to make this as enjoyable for you as I possibly can. I'll be honest, I'm sure it probably isn't. Change isn't enjoyable. But think of it this way. You're changing for the better. Instead of living in Chicago, you can live in California. Be taken care of by a multi-millionaire or whoever buys you. It's a win-win for everyone involved. Bo and I make money. You get to have a lavish lifestyle while giving it up a few times. Embrace the moment. You should be proud that you were picked to be auctioned off. If you were some troll-looking bitch, I would have just walked right by you, but there is something different about you. Call it charm, or radiance, or just natural beauty. You have got it."

"I also have a life back home. Friends. Family. They mean more to me than anything else in the world," said Samantha.

"Great. Maybe someday you'll get to see them again. I don't know. I guess it depends on what your master or owner allows you to do. I'm just saying, think about how great life will be now. Everything you ever want, or need, will be taken care of for you. We're doing you a favor by taking you away from your parents. Really, you should be thanking us."

"I want to go back home," said Samantha.

"If you keep saying that, I swear to God you won't fucking make California. I'll break your goddamn neck right here and leave you on the side of the road," said Carl.

Samantha kept silent.

"Are you hungry?"

"A little."

"We'll stop for lunch in Mobile. I know of a little burger place there that is pretty good. Good Cajun food."

"Okay."

"So, you have any boyfriends yet?" asked Carl.

"No," replied Samantha.

"Good. You ever have sex?"

"No."

"Even better. Kissed a boy or girl?"

"A couple years ago I kissed a boy."

"Anything more than that?"

"No."

"Good. So, you're still a virgin."

Samantha didn't say anything again.

"Look. I appreciate your being honest with me. It helps me understand you better. Why don't you have a boyfriend?"

"I don't know. Just don't."

"Probably not ready for a relationship like that. Or saving yourself for this kind of opportunity. I'll be sure and mention that you're a virgin. That should fetch more at the auction, too. There's a bit more respect among the elite when they know that they are bidding on a virgin. If you were a whore, I would anticipate that you wouldn't get nearly as much."

Samantha kept silent, keeping her thoughts to herself. She looked around the back of the van. The doors, windows, corners, side paneling. She was taking it all in.

"So, what's your favorite food?" asked Carl as the music on the radio changed from Fur Elise to music by Mozart.

"Pizza."

"Nice. I like pizza too. What's your favorite topping?"

"Pineapple."

"Well, everyone has their own preference. How about school? How are you doing there?"

"Fine."

"Good grades?"

"Yeah."

"How long have your parents been together? I saw them back at the airport. They seem together, but distant."

"For as long as I've been alive."

"So, a little more than twelve years. That seems right. How many friends you got back in school?"

"A few."

"Anyone you call your best friend?"

"Emily."

"How old is Emily?"

"She's twelve too."

"Nice. So hey, I'm going to ask you a personal question, is that okay?"

Samantha didn't respond back to Carl.

"Back there at the rest stop, when you were in the bathroom, what did Bo talk to you about?"

"Nothing."

"Bullshit. I could hear someone talking in there. Just couldn't hear what was being said because of the highway noise. Was it you or him talking?"

"Him."

"What was he talking about?"

"Nothing."

"Listen. You're not in trouble. I'm not going to kick the shit out of you for telling me, I just want to know what he was telling you."

"He was talking about getting in trouble."

"What do you mean?"

"A few years ago, he got caught in the shower with his daughter. Said it wasn't his fault."

"What else did he say?"

"That he was married at one time."

"And?"

"And he made me say that I believed him."

"Did he try to touch you?"

"He forced my back up against the wall."

"Why?"

"He wanted me to tell him that it wasn't wrong what he had done."

Carl sat back in his seat, looking around outside the driver's side mirror. Watching the road passing by and vehicles go by.

"Listen to me. I want you to be careful around this guy. He can't keep his own dick under control, you understand me? If something happens and he tries to touch you or do something to you, I want you to let me know. The problem is money doesn't keep his sexual desires under control. Don't get me wrong, he's a hard worker and dependable. But when it comes to keeping his hands off the merchandise, he can't fuckin do it. Do you understand me?"

"Yes."

"While you're in my control, your safety is my one priority. These fuckers in Los Angeles won't pay a fucking dime if you get raped, or cut up, or end up with broken bones. Which means I won't get paid. You see what I mean? So, if something happens, and you get hurt in some way that affects your price this weekend, I'll just kill you myself and start over with the next twelve-year-old. You understand that?" said Carl.

Samantha looked up and made eye contact with him in the rear-view mirror. Her eyes were wet from tearing up.

"I'll take it you understand. You're going to be worth a good chunk of money. Don't lose that for me," said Carl.

The white van continued to drive down the interstate towards Mobile, Alabama. Classical music played over the van speakers for the duration of the drive. Samantha sat quietly in the back of the van, still looking for any weak points in the van for a way out if they stopped. As the hours ticked by, they passed Mobile, Alabama, and crossed the state border into Mississippi.

Samantha noticed that the sun was directly overhead, so it must've been sometime in the afternoon. She didn't have a watch or her cell phone, which she had left back in the hotel room back in Florida.

"I'm going to take the next exit, and we're going to get some lunch. A small burger shack called Hot Damn Burgers. You ever been there?" asked Carl.

"No."

"You ever even hear of it?"

"No."

Carl laughed. "That's okay. You need to be from Mississippi to have heard of it. Even then, only a couple smaller towns in Mississippi have them. Best burger you'll ever have in your life, though. I can promise you that."

The van took the next exit and turned off onto a smaller street in the small town of St. Martin, Mississippi—a small town of almost ten thousand people in the southernmost point of the state in Jackson County. Known as one of the safer communities in all of St. Martin, Carl had no issues sneaking in under the radar and grabbing lunch here. The van drove through the small town until they pulled into Hot Damn Burger's parking lot. Carl parked the van and leaned over to wake Bo up.

"Hey, wake up," he said, nudging his partner.

"What? What is it?" said Bo as he sat up and reoriented himself to the environment.

"Stopping to get lunch. You want something?"

"Hot Damn Burgers?"

"Yeah, what do you want?"

"Swiss melt," he said, going back to sleep in the seat.

"Fucker!" yelled Carl, slapping him with an open hand in the chest. "You need to stay awake while I order and get food."

"Oh, right?"

"So, you want a Swiss melt?"

"Yeah."

Carl leaned back and looked in the back of the van at Samantha.

"What do you want?"

She didn't reply to him.

"Hey! I asked you, what do you want? I'm buying."

"Cheeseburger."

"You allergic to anything I need to know about?"

"No."

"Great. I'll be back. You want fries too?" he asked, looking at Bo.

"Yeah, and their spicy dipping sauce too."

"Fine," said Carl, opening the door. He got out and shut the door behind him, locking it with the keys.

"I was having a good dream too," said Bo, as he leaned his head on his shoulder and drifted back to sleep.

Samantha watched as Carl went up and stood in a small line waiting to order lunch. She also watched Bo fall back asleep in the passenger seat. When she thought he was asleep, she spoke up.

"Bo," she said.

Bo didn't respond to her. He fell back into the deep sleep he had been in before Carl had nudged him awake.

Samantha got on her hands and knees and crawled towards the front of the van, peeking out the front window. She saw Carl standing in line as she heard Bo snore. Samantha looked around the front of the van, past the cooler in between the two front seats on the floorboard. She carefully reached over and opened the glovebox, careful not to wake Bo, but saw nothing of use.

She stood up and sat in the driver's seat of the van. Samantha tried opening the driver's side door and slipping out, but it was locked. Opening the flap that covered the pocket on the side of the door, she looked in and found a flashlight, a pair of pliers, packets of salt, pepper, ketchup and mustard, as well as three different-sized pocketknives. A large knife, a medium-sized knife, and then a smaller knife. She took the smaller knife and opened it. The knife had about an inch and a half blade on it that came to a sharp point, good for poking into things.

She set the small blade back and took out the medium-sized knife and opened it. This knife also came to a point and was about two and a half inches in length. She took this knife and pocketed it. Looking up, she saw Carl ordering food at the window. Moving with care, she crawled into the back of the van again. She took the knife out and tried prying open the padlock keeping the door handles chained. She stopped when she realized the knife couldn't pick the padlock open, though. Folding the knife up, Samantha slipped it back into her pocket and sat down on the hard floor of the van.

A few minutes later, the driver's side of the van opened back up. Carl tossed the food onto the seat of the van as he stood up on the running board, helping himself in. He grabbed the bag of food, sat down in the seat, and closed the door.

"Goddamn it. Bo!" he yelled, shoving his passenger in the shoulder.

"Oh! Hey, I'm sorry I must have fallen back to sleep," said Bo, sitting up in the passenger seat.

"Yeah, no shit! Can't you just stay awake for ten minutes while I go run and grab food?" asked Carl.

"Hey, I'm sorry, man. I didn't mean it."

"Alright, here is your Swiss melt," said Carl, handing him the carryout box of food. "Hey. Here's your cheeseburger," he said, tossing the box into the back of the van for Samantha.

They ate their meals there in the parking lot. Carl ate his cheeseburger quickly, then tossed the garbage in the back with Samantha. He then started the van and drove out of the parking lot, while Bo and Samantha were still eating.

"Did they have any tartar sauce?" asked Bo.

"Tartar sauce? You're eating fries. Not fish, you dumbass," said Carl.

"Have you ever had tartar sauce with your fries before?"

"No. Because tartar sauce is for fish."

"You gotta try it with fries."

"I'm thirsty," said Samantha.

"Jesus Christ, kid," said Bo, reaching into the cooler between the seats and grabbing a water bottle from it.

He tossed the bottle back at Samantha, hitting her in the stomach with the bottle. She picked up the bottle that had fallen to the side of her legs, opened it, and drank.

"I hate the traffic there in Mobile. Glad it's behind us now," said Bo.

"Yeah, it's a bitch, some of those exits on the interstate."

Bo finished the fries from his takeout box and tossed his garbage into the back of the van, where Samantha had finished her bottle of water. She discarded her garbage in the back as well, then quietly she lay down and fell asleep on the cold, hard surface of the van's floor. Carl carried on driving west on Highway 10 as Bo slipped back into a restful sleep, propping his head up against the glass window.

Chapter 8: Cove, Texas

Carl's white van continued its drive down Interstate 10, passing through large towns like Baton Rouge and Lafayette in Louisiana. They crossed over the border into Texas and then through Beaumont. Carl was growing tired of driving as the evening approached. Bo slept in the passenger seat, while Samantha slept on the floor in the back. Driving down the highway, Carl saw an exit sign for the town of Cove, Texas, fast approaching.

Nestled in northwestern Chambers County, Cove, Texas, lies on the western side of Old River Lake, an arm of the Trinity River located west of the town. Home to only 500 residents, the town holds a historical significance as a settlement named for its protected location on Trinity Bay and its historic role in cotton ginning and shipbuilding for the Gulf of Mexico.

Carl leaned over and nudged Bo awake as he was exiting off the interstate, using Exit 803 to enter the small town.

"What do you want?" asked Bo as he sat up in his seat.

"Time to switch. I need a piss break here at the gas station anyway," said Carl as he was off the exit and pulling into a run-down gas station.

He pulled in next to a gas pump and stopped the van. Turning it off, he unbuckled himself from his seat.

"Stay here. I'm going to go inside and piss, then pay for some gas too," said Carl.

"I need to piss too, man," said Bo.

"Wait here until I get back," Carl said as he got out of the van, shutting the door behind him and walking up to the doors of the old station.

While Carl was paying for gas and getting the key to use the bathroom outside the station, Samantha woke up in the back of the van. Realizing that they had come to a stop. She sat up and looked around through the front window. Noticing that the sun was setting in front of them off on the horizon and behind homes and trees.

"What time is it?" asked Samantha.

"Evening," said Bo.

Samantha sat up, propping her back up against the side of the van. Carl returned a short time later, knocking on the passenger side window of the van and motioning for Bo to come out.

Bo jumped out of the van, shutting the door behind him, while Carl walked around the front of the van and to the side where the gas cap was on. He took the nozzle from the gas pump, stuck it into the gas tank and began pumping gas into the van. It wasn't long after he started pumping gas when he heard a knocking on the driver's side window. He looked over and noticed that it was Samantha who was knocking on the window. Carl walked over and cracked the driver's side door open.

"What the hell do you want?" asked Carl.

"I need to use the bathroom," replied Samantha.

"Damn it," he said under his breath as he opened the door for Samantha.

"Get out," he said as Samantha jumped out of the van and onto the cement ground. Carl grabbed her firmly by the arm.

"You make one move to try and get away, and I will kill you. You understand?"

"Yes."

"Come on," said Carl, as he took her by the arm and walked her across the gas station parking lot.

He got close to the bathroom when he saw the bathroom door open and Bo, who was coming out of the small bathroom attached along the side of the old gas station.

"Yo," he said to Bo. "She needs to use the bathroom. Take care of it, then bring her back when she's done."

Carl handed Samantha's arm to Bo, who took her by the arm firmly and walked her into the bathroom together while Carl finished pumping gas. Once inside, Bo locked the door behind them. It was a small eight-foot by eight-foot space, with a dirty porcelain sink, paper towel dispenser and a toilet with no partition walls. The floor was covered in mud, tracked in by occupants who had used it recently. Urine covered the back of the bowl, making it less than sanitary for anyone using it.

"Alright, go. I suppose you want me to turn my back again?" asked Bo.

"Yes, please," said Samantha, who was very embarrassed at having to use the bathroom again with Bo accompanying her. Especially in these conditions. She lowered her pants, sat on the toilet, and waited until she used the toilet.

"You know something?" asked Bo.

Samantha didn't respond to him.

"For a 12-year-old girl, you are very beautiful. I mean, developing in all the right places, have a cute face and eyes. Silky smooth hair. Your skin is soft. You're going to make someone really happy soon," said Bo.

Once again, Samantha didn't respond.

"Listen. I have an idea. It could help us make a little money on the side too. And it's not hard to do either," he said, taking his phone out of his pants pocket.

Bo turned around and took two steps over toward Samantha, showing her his phone that contained pictures of different young girls around her age, naked and in provocative positions.

"Hear me out. With how beautiful you are, we could make some money. You and me. If you just let me take a few pictures while we're here. It would take like five minutes, and five minutes could make us both a lot of money."

"No, I just want to use the bathroom. Please turn around."

"Honey, it'll be quick. Five minutes could make us thousands of dollars. I'll cut you in on the deal too," said Bo as he raised his phone up and took a picture of Samantha sitting on the toilet seat.

"I said no!" yelled Samantha as Bo took a couple more pictures.

"Look, I know you don't know any better! You can't comprehend thousands of dollars, but it's worth it! Believe me! You know what else is worth even more money?" Asked Bo.

"Leave me alone!" yelled Samantha out loud again.

"Let me show you what else is worth even more money," he said, putting his phone back into his pants pocket, then grabbing her by the hair and pushing her down onto the ground in front of the toilet bowl, his back towards the bathroom door now.

Bo held her down forcefully and began to quickly remove his jeans as Samantha yelled, telling him to get off her as he was forcing himself onto her. Samantha pushed back against him, with all her strength trying to push him off her, but she was just not strong enough.

As soon as Bo had unbuckled his belt, unbuttoned his jeans, and unzipped his fly in front of his jeans, he felt a hefty blow to the back of his head. He felt a second blow to the back of his head when he felt his body go numb, and his vision got blurry. He slinked off Samantha, sprawling out on the floor of the bathroom. Samantha yelled again and pushed herself out from under him. Looking up, she saw Carl, who had kicked the bathroom door in and was now standing over Bo.

"You goddamn son of a bitch!" yelled Carl as he stomped the back of Bo's head in with his right foot.

Samantha crawled up against the wall of the bathroom and watched in horror as blood and brain matter spread across the floor and splattered onto the bathroom wall, more viscera added with each violent stomp. Some of it hit Samantha in the face and on her shirt as well. All the while, Carl cursed as he stomped on the back of Bo's head until there was no head left, killing his partner there in the bathroom.

Carl took a step back to regain his composure, shutting the door to the bathroom to hide what had just happened.

"Fucking asshole!" he yelled, breathing hard from the adrenaline rush he had just experienced from brutally murdering his partner.

He looked over at Samantha, who was still lying on the floor. Her pants were partially pulled up to her thighs.

"Get up and put your pants on all the way," he said as he turned to the sink and grabbed some paper towels.

He turned the sink on, drawing out cold water. Wetting the towel, he walked over to Samantha and rubbed the blood and brain matter off her face, cleaning her up. He tossed the used paper towels into the toilet and flushed. Carl then went back to the sink and got more paper towels and wet those when he lost control of his emotions, slamming his fists into the side of the porcelain sink. With each punch into the sink, he uttered curses toward Bo as if he were reliving the moment of killing him. When he finally stopped and controlled his emotions, the bathroom was silent. The sound of running water was all that could be heard.

"Fuck him. The son of a bitch. Could never keep his dick in his pants. I told him. I told him, goddamn it! Not to fuck this up. I told him!" said Carl, still upset over the situation.

Samantha sat on the floor of the dirty bathroom in shock, staring at the lifeless body of the man and the wound inflicted on his body.

Carl wet the paper towels in his hand and then tossed them at Samantha on the floor.

"Wipe your shirt clean as best you can," he said.

She leaned over, picking up the damp paper towels from off the floor. She wiped off the front of her shirt. Carl then leaned over Bo's body, took his wallet from his back pocket and slid it into his pant pocket. He then grabbed Samantha by the arm, pulled her over his body towards the exit. He took a couple of deep breaths and opened the door. Stepping out, he had Samantha by the arm and walked her back over to the van. He opened the passenger-side door and led Samantha inside by the arm.

She got into the van, making her way towards the back as Carl shut and locked the door behind her. He then walked around the front of the van, unlocked the driver's side door and got in. He buckled himself in as Samantha found her place on the floor in the back and sat down, propping her back up against the wall. Carl started the van, then pulled out of the gas station and back onto the road, leaving his partner's body on the gas station's bathroom floor.

"Goddamn bastard," he said as he looked out the driver's side window.

He reached into his pants pocket and pulled out a cell phone. Samantha watched him as he punched in numbers on the phone and, when he had finished dialing, he brought the phone up to his ear and waited for a moment.

"Mr. Harkin. It's Carl. Sir, something happened," said Carl over the phone.

There was a short pause.

"It's Bo. He's dead."

There was another short pause.

"He tried to rape the girl in the gas station bathroom, so I killed him."

After another pause for a moment, Carl spoke into the phone's receiver again.

"No, sir. I stopped him before he could do anything. He had taken her into the bathroom so she could go use it but then forced himself on her when they were in there," said Carl, pausing on the phone again and listening to Mr. Harkin talk.

"No, I don't think there will be any bruising, and like I said, he wasn't able to rape her before I kicked the door in."

There was another pause as Carl stopped talking for a moment.

"I left the body there, sir. I took his wallet from his pocket."

Carl paused again and listened to Mr. Harkin.

"Mr. Harkin, what was I supposed to fucking do? You think people wouldn't look over and see me walking out of the bathroom with a twelve-year-old girl and a headless body? I simply grabbed his wallet, shut the door, and then got into the van and took off. Trying to give myself a good head start before the fucking state patrol show up."

Carl listened intently as Mr. Harkin spoke.

"That's fine, sir. I'm going to need to stay the night with you and get some rest. That fucker was supposed to take over for us and get us to Sonora, but now that won't be possible. Thank you for the car too, sir. Believe me, there won't be any more hookups along the way now."

Carl stopped and listened to Mr. Harkin again.

"Yes, sir. See you in a few hours. We still need to go through Houston and San Antonio. Then it won't be long until we're at your farm in Sonora, sir," said Carl as he hung up his phone, setting it down on the dash of the van.

"Goddamn fucker. I hope he rots in hell," said Carl. "Are you doing okay back there?" he said, looking up and into the back of the van.

Samantha sat with her back propped up against the wall of the van. She had pulled her knees up to her chest and held them with her arms close to her body.

"Hey, I'm talking to you! Are you hurt?" asked Carl.

"No," she quietly replied to him.

"Good. Wouldn't get any money for you if you were bruised or cut up. We're about four hours from Sonora, and it looks like I'm driving nonstop all the way there. So do the right thing and just lay down back there and go to sleep. Are you thirsty?

"No."

"Alright, just sit back there and go to sleep then."

Samantha was tired. She knew it. She didn't want to shut her eyes, though. Every time she did, she saw Bo, who tried to do what he did, then Carl killing him in the bathroom in front of her. The blood splashed up onto her shirt and face as she sat on a wet, urine-soaked gas station bathroom floor. But she was tired enough that she was starting to get a headache from not sleeping enough. Eventually, she laid down with her back turned towards Carl, who was driving down the interstate and getting closer to Houston. A few tears rolled down her face as she closed her eyes and dreamed nightmares of her experiences over the past few days now.

*   *   *   *

"Gas station attendant said he found him like that, ma'am," said a Texas Highway Patrolman, as he walked back to his patrol vehicle.

Parked next to the vehicle was his sergeant for the evening, Sergeant Linda Brumley. Seargent Brumley, who was outside of her patrol vehicle, was waiting for the young patrolman to come back to his car to let her know what the attendant had said.

"So, he found him like that in the bathroom. Fucking head smashed in like a goddamn pumpkin. Thinks the body hasn't been there for over twenty minutes at the most. He went out looking for the key to the bathroom, because people never return it when they use it, and that's when he found the body. This job never gets any easier."

"He got any surveillance video?" asked Sergeant Brumley.

"He does, but only of the inside of the convenience store. Nothing on the pumps, or the bathroom," said the patrolman, reaching into his back pocket and removing a can of chew. He opened the can, stuffing a wad of chew into the bottom of his lip.

"I told you; you need to quit chewing that shit. It's not healthy for you."

"Yeah, my wife says that too," he said as he spat on the ground.

"This isn't going to be our investigation."

"Whose investigation is it going to be if not ours?"

"Texas Rangers, it sounds like."

"Well, fuck it, didn't really feel like doing an investigation on this one, anyway. You should go in there and see that bathroom. Shit all over the walls. Piss on the floors. Then, the body of course. Are the Rangers on their way here?"

"Two of them are. Got off the phone with them while you were in there taking a statement from the attendant."

"Well, before they get here, you should go have a look. It's a real shitshow in that bathroom. Literally."

"I'd rather not."

"Oh, come on. When was the last time you saw a person's head completely smashed into the ground like a pancake?"

"Can't say I ever have."

"Well, this is your chance," said the patrolman, spitting on the ground again.

"Fucking dirty habit," said Sergeant Brumley. "I'm going to go talk to the attendant inside. Let him know that the Rangers will probably want a statement from him, too."

"Yeah, he's not too sure who it could be. Doesn't recognize the clothes the guy is wearing. Sounds like the stiff never came into the store."

"I'll go talk to him."

"Well, good luck. On the way back, check out the body, too."

Sergeant Brumley walked away from the patrol cars and the patrolman, who spat again on the ground. She crossed the parking lot. Opening the door to the convenience store, she walked inside. The Middle Eastern man was short in stature, in his late 50s and had short silver hair. He wore a plaid blue button-up shirt and a pair of khaki pants.

"Are you Amir?" she asked.

"Yes, ma'am," he replied with a thick accent.

"Where is your family from?"

"Somalia."

"Cool. Were you born here in the country or did you immigrate here from Somalia?"

"Immigrated, ma'am. My son was the first in our family to be born here in the States."

"How long have you been here for?"

"Seventeen years."

"Well. I'd say welcome to America, but you've been here long enough you've probably seen shit wilder than this."

"Not as wild as this is turning out to be, ma'am."

"You got video of the station?"

"Just the inside."

"And you have nothing on the gas pumps?"

"Ma'am, have you seen how old those pumps are? I'm lucky they are still working. God forbid if one broke down, I wouldn't be able to afford the replacement. And you want me to afford an outdoor security system?" he said, sitting down on a stool behind the counter.

"What does your video look like inside the station?"

"Well, come here. Let me show you," he said, standing back up and ushering her behind the counter and back into his office.

A computer with a monitor sat on a desk, displaying a single camera feed from the back of the store, which focused on the counter, front door, and store windows.

"That camera sees the parking lot some. Did you see anyone come in that was suspicious to you?"

"I've seen dozens of folks come in here this evening. They all look suspicious to me, ma'am."

"You see anyone come into the store here dressed like that body you found in the bathroom?"

"No, ma'am."

"Well, thanks for your help. The Texas Rangers are on their way down here. They're going to take control of the investigation going forward," said the sergeant as she walked out of the store, back outside the station.

She paused for a moment outside the front doors of the store and looked around, then walked around the corner of the building, towards the bathroom.

She nudged the bathroom door open, revealing a human body lying on the ground in a large pool of blood, mixed with urine. The head was completely smashed into the ground, and blood was splattered on the wall, trickling down, leaving red lines stained on the white walls mixed with what looked to her to be smeared feces on the wall, too.

Sergeant Brumley stepped into the bathroom and looked around the small room, then down at the body. She looked at the man's back pocket of his jeans, which at one time had the crease in the fabric to show that he had kept his wallet in the right back pocket of the jeans. However, there was no wallet there now. She looked along his side and noticed that there was a square bulge in his left pant pocket. She reached into her garrison belt and got into a pouch she wore on the belt. Inside the pouch were latex gloves. She put one on her right hand and then leaned down. Reaching into his pocket, she grabbed onto a device and pulled it out.

It was a cell phone.

"You know you're stepping all over evidence there, sergeant," said a voice behind her in the bathroom doorway.

She stood up quickly and turned around to see two men standing in the doorway. One man with a gold badge strapped to the breast pocket of his button-up shirt, while the other wore his badge on his belt.

"Gentlemen, I take it you two are from the Texas Rangers, yes?" she asked.

"Yes, ma'am. Sergeant James, and this is Detective Ho," he said. "What did you find there?"

"A cell phone."

"Anything else?"

"Just a lot of blood and a head smashed into the ground like a pancake. Urine and shit. That's about it."

"Have you talked to the store clerk yet?"

"Yes, sir. Amir is his name. He can't tell who it is. Doesn't recognize the clothes that the deceased is wearing."

"Security video?"

"One camera. Set up inside the store. Looks on the front counter, doors, and windows."

"Nothing on the pumps?"

"Nothing on the pumps."

"Have you viewed the video yet?"

"No."

"Any idea how long the deceased has been here for?"

"Amir told my patrolman he thinks for only a short time."

"What's a short time?"

"Twenty minutes."

"Then how long did it take for you guys to respond?"

"An additional fifteen minutes."

"Then half an hour for us to get out here. So the murder could be a little over an hour away. Who knows in what direction at this point?"

"Well, you're welcome to take a look at the surveillance video," said Sergeant Brumley as she stepped out of the bathroom, past the two Texas Rangers. "I'm going to head back in there to have a look myself."

Linda looked over and called for her patrolman to come back over to the bathroom.

"Scott, keep an eye on the bathroom and rope the scene off until the coroner comes out for the body. Radio me if they show up and we're not back out here yet."

"Yes, ma'am," said Scott as he spat the wad of chew out onto the ground.

"Alright, Linda," said Sergeant James. "How have you been doing? How long have you been a sergeant with the Highway Patrol for now?"

"Not too bad. Became a sergeant shortly after you left six years ago for the Texas Rangers," replied Linda as they walked together back to the front doors of the store.

"Oh, good for you," said Sergeant James, as the two, along with Detective Ho, walked back to the convenience store.

Sergeant James held the door open for both Detective Ho and Linda. They walked inside and met the owner of the shop there at the register, who was finishing up a sale with a customer.

"Hello Amir. I'm Sergeant Alexander James. This is Detective Huy Ho. We are from the Texas Rangers organization," said James, showing his badge to Amir, along with Detective Ho. "Of course, you remember Sergeant Linda Brumley; she is with the Texas Highway Patrol. We'd like to ask you a few more questions if you have a moment."

"Yes, sure."

"You have surveillance video of the store here, yes?"

"Yes, sir. But it's just inside the store."

"Can we see it?"

"Sure, but I don't know what you're going to see. There are no cameras out on the pumps, or in the back on the bathroom either."

"That's fine, I'd like to look at the last two hours of video, please."

"No problem. Follow me to my office," said Amir as he welcomed all three of the officers back to his office.

When they were all inside the owner's office, Amir sat in the chair for a moment and with a couple of clicks of his mouse, he retrieved video for the past two hours of the inside of the gas station.

"So, the door to the bathroom is locked, Amir?" asked Linda.

"Yes, it is. I had to give the key to the man who came in and bought gas."

"Did you get the key back from him?" asked Detective Ho.

"No, I never did."

"You think that might be the murderer?" asked Linda.

"Hard to tell. But it could be a start. You remember what he was wearing or what he looked like?"

"Yeah, he was a middle-aged man, balding. Looked like he hadn't shaved for a couple of days. He wore bifocals and was wearing a purple windbreaker jacket and old faded blue jeans. Black sneakers, too."

"Skinny guy?"

"Yeah, he was. Not like he was anorexic. But more athletic."

"Was he wearing any jewelry you could see when he was in here? Tattoos?"

"Not that I could see, no. I'm sorry, you guys. I'm the only one here, and I need to help some customers who are waiting for me. You're welcome to continue reviewing the video. It's a very basic system. Play features are in the corner of the screen. Play, pause, reverse, fast forward," he said as he walked out of the office.

Seargent James sat down in the chair in the office, as Linda and Detective Ho watched behind his shoulder.

"Do you guys notice something here?" he asked.

"No, what?"

"We can still see out the window. It's very faint. But you can see vehicles pulling up to the pumps on the side closest to the front of the store."

Linda squinted and looked at the screen and noticed that he was right. They could see the vehicles that were pulling up to the gas pumps closest to the windows and the front of the store. The three watched as a few vehicles came and went.

Finally, they saw a white van pull up to the gas pumps. A moment later, the driver stepped out of the van and walked into the gas station. He was a middle-aged man who matched the description Amir had given. The man paid for something, then Amir gave him the keys to the bathroom. The balding man with the purple windbreaker walked out and around the corner of the station, looking toward the bathroom.

"That looks like that's the guy that Amir had described to us before," said Detective Ho.

"It sure as hell does," said Linda, as they continued to watch the screen.

A short time later, he walked back out to the white van parked at the gas pumps.

"If he really used the bathroom, then he would have said something if there was a dead body in that bathroom," said Sergeant James.

They continued watching the video and saw the man walk up to the passenger-side door. Another man opened the passenger door and jumped out of the van, dressed similarly to the dead body on the floor of the bathroom. The man handed this man something and then walked around the opposite side of the van and disappeared for a bit. The man who jumped out of the passenger side of the van shut the passenger door and walked towards the bathroom.

"That sure looks like our victim, does it not?" asked Linda.

"Looks like the same shirt," said Detective Ho.

They continued to watch the monitor until, a short time later, they saw the man who was pumping gas walk around the front of the van, but this time with a third person with him. A shorter person, holding their arm as they walked them across the parking lot, behind the building again and out of camera view.

"Who the hell is that third person?" asked Seargent James to himself and the group.

"Short woman?" asked detective Ho.

"Maybe a young girl," said Linda.

"So, two men and a young girl? Or a short woman," said Sergeant James.

They continued to watch the monitor and watched as one man came back to the van a moment later after disappearing out of camera view by himself.

"Where's the small woman?" asked Linda.

"I don't know. She's in the bathroom or waiting by the bathroom, maybe?"

The first man walked back over to the van and around the corner to where the gas tank was. They assumed he resumed pumping gas, and a short time later they saw him get into the van for a moment. They watched as he sat in the van for a few minutes, then got out and walked across the parking lot. Back towards where the bathroom was behind the store. He then disappeared from the camera's view.

"Goddamn it, this guy needs to get more cameras here at this gas station," said Sergeant James.

"Cameras cost money. You see how old those pumps are out front? He's lucky he can even afford one for inside the store. Insurance probably requires him to put one up on the register," said Linda.

They watched intently. Sergeant James watched the seconds tick by, one second after another, anticipating what would come next. A short time after the man disappeared out of camera view, he returned into camera view, dragging the short woman by the arm before he opened the passenger door and pulled her up into the van. Shutting the door behind her, he hurried around the front of the white van and got in. The vehicle started and took off from the gas station. They weren't even able to see in which direction the vehicle had gone.

"He left," said Detective Ho.

"He did. Without the second man," said Linda.

"I guarantee you that's our killer. Linda, you said you found that phone on the deceased. Does that phone still have battery power?" asked Sergeant James.

She looked at the phone in her hand. Turning it on, she looked in the corner of the screen.

"Says twenty-seven percent," she said.

"That's enough. Are there any phone calls or texts that you can see on there?" asked Sergeant James.

She tried unlocking the phone but couldn't get past the four-digit code.

"There's a passcode. I can't access it without bricking this phone and locking it permanently."

"Can you access the pictures at least?"

"That I can," said Linda, as she accessed the photo album on the phone without unlocking it.

"Holy shit," she said as she scrolled through the picture album on her phone.

"What? What is it?"

"Child pornography."

"What?"

"Child pornography. I would guess young girls. Pre-teens and early teens. Some half naked. Some naked."

"I can't imagine this guy had it coming to some degree then. Anything recent?"

"Yeah. Today," said Linda.

"What does it show?" Asked detective Ho as he looked down on the screen as Linda flipped through the current photos.

"The bathroom here in at the gas station. Plus, a girl sitting on the toilet. Trying to relieve herself, it looks like."

"That's the short woman we saw the one man walk across the parking lot."

"She's not a short woman. She's a young girl. Looks like she's a young teenager? At the most. He took five pictures of her. All sitting on the toilet with her pants around her thighs. This one she's looking up in the photo."

"What the hell is she doing traveling with these two?"

"Maybe she's related to them?"

"Maybe. Seems like a weird set of photos to have of your daughter or niece like that though. Whatever relation she is to them. Anything else?"

"No. Just those five pictures. Then a bunch of child pornography after that. Boy and girl. Fucking disgusting," she said, turning the phone off in disgust.

"Huy, do you have an evidence bag with you?" asked Sergeant James.

Detective Ho reached into the inside of his jacket pocket, pulling out a Ziplock evidence bag. He opened it while Linda put the phone into the bag. He then zipped the bag shut and took possession of the phone from Linda.

"Sorry you had to be the one that found that, Linda. I know that's not an easy thing to see."

"It's part of the job. I can accept it," said Linda.

"Well, Detective Ho, I think we need to see if we can get a recording of this security video. Can you coordinate with the owner and make sure we get that collected for our case?" asked Sergeant James.

"Sure," replied Detective Ho as he turned around and left the office with the phone.

"So, Linda. Do you ever think about leaving the highway patrol? Coming to work for the Texas Rangers?" said Sergeant James, standing up from the chair at the desk and turning to walk towards the office door.

"You know, I gave it some thought, and I'm too loyal to the highway patrol at the moment," said Linda in reply.

"Well, when they finally piss you off enough, you're welcome to come and apply with us. You're a good officer, Linda. I think you'd make a good detective with us too."

"Thanks. I'll keep the offer in mind. So, what is the plan here?" she asked him as they left the office and walked back out into the market towards the front doors.

"Well, we'll take that phone back to our forensics office. Drop it off there. See what we can get out of it. As far as the girl goes, I don't know. She could be related. She might not be."

"Think you should check lost and missing children in the area?"

"Yeah, we could certainly look at the database we've got. But who knows who she is just yet. I'm more interested in tracking down a murderer at this point. Would be a child predator of some kind too, if he weren't already dead on the floor of a gas station bathroom," said Sergeant James, as the two walked around the back corner of the gas station together, back towards the bathroom, where Linda's patrolman was waiting for them.

"Sergeant Brumley. The coroner will be here in half an hour to take possession of the body. I got the area roped off while you guys were in the building too," said the patrolman, reaching into his back pocket again for a can of chew.

"That's a dirty habit, kid. You should quit that shit while you still can," said Sergeant James.

"Ain't the first time I've heard that," he said, opening the lid and sticking a wad of chew into the bottom of his lip again.

Detective Ho left the gas station, walked around the corner of the building and towards the group of officers standing by the bathroom.

"He's going to record the video onto a compact disk for us to have," he said.

"Sounds good to me. Take some photos of the scene and have a look around while you still can. The coroner will be here in about half an hour. Said his sergeant."

Detective Ho got to work. Going to the Ranger's vehicle and getting into the trunk to retrieve an evidence kit and digital camera, he took pictures of the scene and gathered evidence. Because of the environment, most of the evidence was contaminated with human waste and garbage as the can in the bathroom had also been knocked over in the scuffle between the murderer and the victim. When he had finished collecting what he could, the coroner of Chambers County arrived with his truck.

He took control of the physical scene when the Texas Rangers gave him the okay to do so. Taking possession of the body and with the help of the Rangers, he placed the body into a body bag, then placed it onto a gurney he had brought out of the back of the truck. Pushing the gurney to the back of the truck, he slid it into the bed of the truck, then shut the tailgate.

"Well, that's all there is to it," said the coroner. "I tell you what. I'm not sure you're going to need an autopsy to figure out how this guy died."

"We still would like one. Toxicology specifically. I would like to see if there are any drugs or alcohol in his system," said Detective Ho.

"Alright, you've got it. Give it a couple of days and I'll be sure and get a report over to you guys."

Sergeant James took a business card out of his pocket, along with Detective Ho, handing them over to the coroner. He took them, wished them well, and got back into his truck with the deceased in the back and drove out. Sergeant James wished Linda well as he and Detective Ho got back in their vehicle as well and left the scene. Meanwhile, Linda went back into the store. She told Amir that they were finished with their investigation and that the bathroom was his to do what he wanted with it. Both Linda and her patrolman left the shop and went back to their vehicles to leave.

"What are you thinking, ma'am?" asked the patrolman.

"You want to know what I think?" she said in reply as she opened the driver's side door to her patrol vehicle. "I think there is more to this scene than meets the eye. I don't think it's just a murder."

"What do you mean?"

Linda didn't respond to his question but gave him a look as she sat down in her patrol car.

"I think there's more to that girl than meets the eye is what I mean," she said to herself as she put the car in gear and drove out of the gas station parking area.

Chapter 9: Sonora, Texas

"Shit, I am so damn tired," said Carl, as he squeezed the bridge of his nose between his right index finger and thumb.

The white van rolled past Junction, Texas—a small town almost two hours outside the city limits of San Antonio, tucked along the quiet stretch of Interstate 10. With a population of almost 3,000 people, it wasn't the kind of place travelers lingered. Ranch land sprawled beyond the roadside, and the heart of the town pulsed through family businesses and generations-old homesteads. The kind of place where strangers stood out, making Junction the wrong place for a stop.

Carl looked down at his phone, turning the GPS function on and looking at his route. He saw that the drive to Sonora and the chicken farm was now less than an hour away.

"Thank God," he said under his breath as he turned his phone off and set it down on the dash of the van.

"I need to go to the bathroom," said Samantha from the back of the van.

"You're just going to have to hold it in until we get to the farm," said Carl.

"I'm thirsty, too."

"Yeah, you and me both. That I can do for you," said Carl, as he leaned over and opened the cooler between the two front seats.

He grabbed a bottle of water, tossing it into the back of the van. Samantha got up on her hands and knees and crawled over to the back corner of the van where the bottle came to rest. Carl then grabbed a bottle of water for himself, opened it, and drank about half the bottle.

"We're about an hour away from Sonora. Maybe forty-five minutes now. It won't be long before we're there."

Samantha didn't respond.

"I'm sorry you had to see that back there in Cove. In the gas station bathroom. Bo was a different cat. I know what he was doing to the kids we were catching and taking to this auction in California. I've seen the pictures on his phone, and I'm sure there were a couple that he had his way with too. He was just a bad dude."

"I think you're both ugly," replied Samantha after taking a sip of water.

"Come now. It's not like that at all. Samantha, you know why I do what I do? Why do I catch children like you to sell at these auctions? Well, I don't sell them. I just catch the kids, and Mr. Harkin sets up the sales. But anyway, you know why I do what I do?"

"I don't care."

"That's fine. I know I'm not a good person. I'll be the first to admit that I'm a real piece of shit. I never amounted to much growing up. As a kid or as a young adult. As a kid, I was always getting in trouble. Bad grades in school. Fighting with my parents. Starting fights in the neighborhood. Stealing shit. I went through an arson period, but I never got caught for that. Then, I turned seventeen and ran away from home. I was married for a bit, but that didn't last for very long either. In my early twenties, I was back out on the road. Never divorced her," said Carl, laughing to himself. "So I suppose I'm still married? Hell, I don't know how that works.

Anyway, I met this guy you're about to meet here soon. Mr. Harkin. He gave me work to do at this chicken farm as a manager there. Led a crew of workers from Mexico who worked on the farm, while he handled the business side of things. One day Mr. Harkin calls me into his farmhouse, and we're sitting at the table, and he talks to me about human trafficking and how it can pay the bills better than selling chicken eggs. I was a little hesitant about it at first, but he had some good connections in Los Angeles, and we had the opportunity of getting labor from Mexico, and those fathers have daughters, you know? Finally, we just ran out of girls to sell, so then I started kidnapping kids. Hired Bo a few years back, who helped traffic kids to California too, but he was a pedophile. I knew he was. Then he started showing me child porn he had on his phone and some things that he recorded himself doing with kids. He thought I got off on that shit too, but I always found it disgusting. I told him time and time again never to fuck around with the kids that we kidnap. The money is more important than satisfying your own sick bullshit. But I'm certain he had. I just never could catch him doing it with the kids we had kidnapped. Until today. So, I suppose what you saw tonight was a couple of years' worth of anger and frustration, dealing with his sick bullshit. It wasn't your fault what happened back there."

"How many children have you done this to?" asked Samantha.

"Kidnapped? Twenty-two. Sold into sex work? Nineteen."

"What happened to the other two?"

"They fought back, so I dealt with them and started over, finding new children."

"What do you mean you dealt with them?"

"I killed them. Buried them out in the desert. In fact, one of their graves we just passed outside of San Antonio on a private dirt road."

"That's not okay."

"I don't really give a shit. Which is why I'm telling you, don't make me make you the third. I don't mind making you my third, but I'd honestly rather have the money from your sale."

Carl cleared his throat, took another drink from his water bottle.

"Mr. Harkin will have a second kid that we're picking up at his farm. Apparently around the same age and developing in all the right places like you are. Just between the two of you, I wouldn't be surprised if we could fetch close to $100,000 total."

"How did he come across her then?"

"He traffics in forced labor from Mexico. You wouldn't believe how many parents from that shithole country are quick to sell their kids to American farms. Not just in Texas too, but all across the country. On occasion, they will sell a kid that he thinks we could send to LA to this house around Hollywood that he thinks can fetch us some good cash in sex work."

"How many children are sold to him?"

"In what, a year?"

"Sure."

"Shit, I'd say Forty. Fifty. Something like that."

"What happens when they get too old to work for him then?"

"Well, he has connections to government officials down in Nigeria. I guess they'll turn around, buy those boys. Once they get them, they will turn around and sell to Boco Haram, that fuckin terrorist group down there and they'll turn the boys into soldiers or if you want to call them that on their front lines of their holy war or whatever nonsense they believe in. So ultimately, they just aren't worth anything anymore on the farm, so Mr. Harkin sells them for whatever he can get for them. Don't ask me how he knows these two officials from Nigeria. The hell if I know, but when they're gone, they're gone."

"Why doesn't he just release them back home to go back to their families?"

"And not get anything for it? Sure, if the parents could pay for them to come back, I suppose. Most of them can't afford what they are worth, and he can't just let them go for free, so he gets whatever he can for the boys through other means. For the girls, they usually go into prostitution. He knows some pimps around the country, and he'll send the girls to them when they can't work on the farm anymore, and they'll go into prostitution until they just aren't usable anymore. Then the pimps can do whatever they want with them. Sometimes that terrorist group will buy the girls, and they'll use them as prostitutes, and that'll help fund their group too. Gotta squeeze out any dime you can get from them to I suppose. And then on the rare occasion, he buys a girl from a Mexican family that he thinks he could get more for selling at these parties in LA than he could getting labor from them as kids, and then payment as prostitutes in their teens and young adult years."

"And that's where we're going?"

"That's right. See where you're going, and you don't have to worry about being a prostitute. Neither will this girl we're picking up. You two will be going to an elite party in LA, just outside of Hollywood, where you're going to be auctioned off to be some rich, horny old fuck's wife. You won't see prostitution or be taken out of the country. Unless I suppose these men retire and move out of the country. Then I guess you'll be moving out of the country. But there's a good chance that won't happen."

"And you think that's okay?"

"I honestly don't give a shit if it's okay. You know how hard it is to make a decent living in this shithole country now? Can't even go to McDonald's and get a meal for one fucking person under twenty dollars these days. How about that? So as long as the money is easy, and the money is good for one, I've got no other choice, and second, I really don't give a shit. I'm just watching out for my best interests."

Samantha leaned back against the inside of the van. She felt the vibration of the vehicle in her back as she tucked her chin into her chest and brought her knees up to her chest and held herself.

"I suppose what they say is true. Human beings are the scariest of monsters," said Carl as he looked forward, driving the van down the interstate.

They left the bright lights of San Antonio behind, now swallowed by the darkness of the Texas desert. Carl yawned a couple times before he turned on the radio and started listening to his classical music. Samantha drifted off to sleep. The lights of oncoming traffic illuminated the inside of the van and she could see Carl in the driver's seat, occupied with driving at the moment. Her eyes were heavy and before she knew it, she was falling asleep there in the back of the van.

*   *   *   *

Waking up in her own living nightmare, Samantha looked around the back of the van, disturbed when she realized the van had already come to a complete stop. She made her way to the front of the van and saw Carl through the windshield speaking with someone. He looked over and noticed that Samantha was in the front seat of the van, looking out at him and this other person. He came around to the passenger side of the van and unlocked the door. Opening it he gestured for Samantha to come out of the van with his hand.

"Come on out here, I want you to meet someone," said Carl.

Samantha slowly stepped out of the van and onto the ground. Down into grass and dirt. She noticed large barns built next to one another. The moonlight lit the grounds around her, and she was able to clearly see the barns and smaller shacks around the grounds.

"Don't you want to hold my arm?" she asked Carl.

"No need. You're not going to go anywhere around here. The desert is in all four directions. Nearest house around these parts are miles away. You're not going anywhere. Come, say hi to this gentleman," Carl said, walking towards the man around the front of the van.

Samantha followed behind, then stood next to Carl.

"Samantha, I would like for you to meet Mr. Harkin. Mr. Harkin, this is Samantha," said Carl.

"Oh, yes. I see what you saw in her. The girl from Chicago, yes?" asked Mr. Harkin.

"Yes, that's right. Flew down to Miami to the Crystal Mountain Resort with her parents."

"Mmm. She is developing in all the right places. How old are you, honey?"

"Twelve, sir."

"Twelve years, old. Wow. Well, you will fetch a decent chunk of cash in the auction this Friday night. You pick them good, Carl."

"Just do what I need to do to bring us in a profit."

"You're a good worker," said Mr. Harkin as he turned and walked away from the van, back towards the two-level home there on the property. There was a large two-level garage next to the home as well that he, Carl and Samantha now walked towards.

"Now that you killed your partner, I'm sure the fucking police will be looking into the matter. If that gas station had cameras, I'm sure they are aware of the van and probably caught you on camera, too. So now we need to disguise you as best as we can. While you're here you can get some fresh clothes. Shave for God sakes, you look like a damn bum. Then we'll get you a new vehicle to continue on to California."

"What of the second girl here you want me to take?"

"No need. I sold her to someone I know who was looking for a wife. Friend of mine from business school. More or less to get back at his fiancée. Well, ex-fiancée now."

"This is all your show. Whatever you want to do with them."

"I never really liked Bo though to be honest with you. When I heard that he was a child molester, I wasn't generally interested in doing business with him anymore. So really you did me a favor, smashing his head into piss and shit in a gas station bathroom floor. Did you grab his wallet and cell phone?"

"His wallet, yes. His cell phone is in the van."

"Oh. Go back and grab it. I want to dispose of it properly before it ends up in someone else's hands that doesn't need to have it," said Mr. Harkin.

Carl turned around and walked the short distance back to the van while Samantha stood there with Mr. Harkin.

"You know this isn't necessarily a bad thing, Samantha. Think of it this way. You won't have to go to school anymore. You'll be taken care of someone rich and wealthy. Wealthier than your own parents."

"I like school. And wealth doesn't make me happy. My friends and my family make me happy."

Mr. Harkin looked up as he heard Carl yell as he slammed the van to the door. He walked back towards him and Samantha.

"It's not in there." He said.

"What do you mean it's not in there?" Asked Mr. Harkin.

"The fuckin phone isn't in the fuckin van!" said Carl, voice shaking with nerves.

"Oh great. That's just great. Shit!" said Mr. Harkin as he turned around and walked back to the garage next to the house.

"Fucking shit!" he yelled again.

"I'm sorry, Mr. Harkin. That son of a bitch must have had it with him in the bathroom with her."

"It's fine. It's fine," said Mr. Harkin. "It'll be fine. All we need to do is come up with a plan. I know some political folks here in Texas. I'll be fine myself. It's just going to cost me a little. Goddamn you, Carl! How fucking stupid can you be to not take the phone from him?"

"I thought he had left it in the van, sir. I'm sorry," said Carl.

"Fine. It's fine. Come on, we really need to get that van hidden now. Take the girl to shack number five. There are a couple of extra beds in there that aren't being used at the moment. Lock her in with the rest of the Mexican children and then drive that van over towards the garage. We're going to have to take it out, deep into the desert, and burn that damn thing," said Mr. Harkin, handing him a key chain with a set of keys on it. He thumbed through the keys on the chain, selected one, and handed it to Carl.

"Yes, Mr. Harkin," said Carl, as he took the keys and Samantha by the arm again and walked her away, over towards the worker shacks on the property.

He guided Samantha toward two rows consisting of a few dozen small wooden shacks, stopping at shack number five in the front row. Carl unlocked the door and opened it, pushing Samantha into the shack.

"Find a bed and sleep here for the night. I'll be back in the morning to come pick you up and we'll take off early," said Carl as he shut the door behind her and locked it.

Inside, Samantha saw six twin sized beds in the small twenty by twenty-foot shack. In four of the beds, she saw young Mexican boys lying down. A couple had woken up from the commotion of Samantha being shoved inside. They looked and watched her for a moment. Two of the boys remained asleep.

Samantha took another step towards one of the beds where one Mexican boy was awake and looking at her.

"Hi," she said.

"Hola," said the boy.

"Do you speak English?" asked Samantha.

"No habla engles?" said the boy, confused.

Samantha could tell he was about her age, too.

"I speak English," said the second boy who was awake in his bed. He looked a little bit older than her.

"Where are we right now?" she asked him, walking over to his bed, which was a twin sized stained spring mattress set up on the floor with an old flat pillow and dirty blanket on top.

The boy pushed the blanket off himself and swung his legs out of the bed, sitting up on the side.

"Chicken farm. We harvest eggs here at this farm. There are thousands of chickens here. Dozens of us. We were all bought last summer from our parents. Some of us from Tijuana. Some from Mazatlán. Some from Mexico City. What we all have in common apart from being from Mexico is that our families were poor and thought that by selling us to men who took us up to Ojinaga, at the border, that they could get out of debt. A lot of our families are in debt to the cartel. Whether they got enough money from the man who owns the chickens to pay off their debts, I do not know."

"So, your parents sold you?"

"Si. To some men who took us up to the Mexican town of Ojinaga. They met some men who worked with the patrolmen there at the border, who took us to a quiet place in the desert off the main road, where the chicken man paid them. Then paid the men who took us up to the border. When they were paid, the border men let us cross over with the chicken man, then we got into a couple white vans and they drove us up here to the farm where we've been working, collecting eggs, feeding chickens, and cleaning the barns and property."

"How long have you been here for?"

"This is our second summer here."

"Will you ever see your mom or dad again?"

"I don't plan on it."

"What do you mean?"

"Last year there was a boy here who was almost seventeen years old. He had worked here on the farm for five summers. Miguel was his name. He came from Cancun and was sold to the chicken man directly from his parents. But he worked here for five summers, then one day the chicken man took him out to the white van and drove him out of here and we haven't seen him since."

"Where did they take him?"

"The chicken man knows a lot of people. People who are in high class and all over the country. He knows people outside of the country too. I found out that Miguel was sold to some men from Boko Haram."

"To who?"

"Boko Haram. They're a terrorist group from Africa I think. More than likely that's where I'll be going too. The chicken man knows some men who he sells to, and they take us and make us fight for them. Sometimes he will sell girls who are old enough too and they'll be used by them, but I'm not sure how. I don't think they are turned into soldiers. But that is the life that we have to look forward to."

"Can you run away?"

"There is nowhere to run around here. Then when were finally moved out of here, there's nowhere to run there too. We can't get away from anyone."

"So, you're just never going to see your parents ever again?"

"That's how it works. It was always meant to be this way anyway. It's my way of giving back to them and giving them the chance to settle their debts with the cartels."

Samantha looked around at the other boys. They were all either around her age or a little younger than she was.

"How old are you?" she asked.

"Sixteen. This will probably be my last summer here, then I'll be sold to Boko Haram."

"I'm sorry."

"Come. You are probably very tired. Did you just get here?"

"I did. Not that long ago. I've been sleeping in the back of a van for a couple nights now."

"Well, have this bed. It's the best one that we have here. Less springs have come out of the mattress and the pillow isn't as stained as the others are," said the boy, giving up his bed to Samantha.

He stood up from the bed and walked away, to the corner where a different, but older mattress lay flat on the dirt ground. He bent down and lay on the mattress.

"Thank you. You don't have to do that."

"It's perfectly fine. I can take this bed here," the boy said.

"What's your name?"

"Mateo."

"That's a nice name."

"It my country it means a gift from God. What's your name?"

"Samantha."

"That's a very pretty name too," said Mateo, with a smile on his face.

"Do you miss your parents?"

Mateo thought for a moment, then answered her question.

"I did at first, yes."

"But not now?"

"I still think about them, but I've come to accept the fact that I'll never see them again. I'm glad to have got to know them while I was still a young boy."

"How did they get into trouble?"

"Debt? With the cartels?"

"What's a cartels?"

"The cartel. They are local gangs that run drugs around the country and outside the country too here into America, South America, I think even into Canada and Europe too."

"So how did they get in trouble with them?"

"My dad did. Mom is just in trouble because she's together with him. But it was mostly dad's fault from what I understand. I don't know all the details though. Mom would never share with me."

"My mom would never tell me when my dad was in trouble too," said Samantha.

"Either way, you probably want to get some rest. Sounds like you haven't had a good night's sleep for a few days."

"Yeah, I haven't."

"How did you come to be here?"

"My mom, dad and I were on a vacation in Florida and one of the men who brought me here kidnapped me from the park we were at. I don't know if I'm ever going to see them again to be honest. Especially hearing your story now."

"You have more hope than I have. More than likely, they are taking you to California."

"Yeah, I've heard them talk about that."

"Listen. The chicken man doesn't know I speak and understand English. So I hear them talk a lot. Where they are taking you is to the Wine and Dine house."

"The what?"

"Wine and Dine house. It's a big home in Los Angeles. Outside of Hollywood. A lot of high-class men and sometimes women will go there to purchase girls for themselves."

"To do what with?"

"I'd imagine marriage. Sex. Partnership. I don't know, whatever they buy girls for. But a lot of big-time businessmen, movie stars, and sometimes some athletes. They are high-class. Really rich. Again, the chicken man knows a lot of people, so as long as he keeps providing girls, the Wine and Dine will stay in business for them."

"I just want to get back to my family."

"Maybe you might someday. Maybe you won't. I don't know. All I know is my future and my future will probably end up being dead in the desert with a rifle by my side."

"I'm sorry to hear that. You should try and run away."

"Won't make a difference. The nearest town is twenty-four miles to the south. It'd take me hours to get there on foot. If the desert didn't kill me, surely the chicken man would for running away. Anyway, it's late and I need some rest. The sun will rise soon, and I need some rest for my work tomorrow. We start working nonstop when the light breaks in the sky, until the sun goes down and sometimes into the night, too. I hope that's not the case tomorrow. I need some rest."

"I'm sorry, I'll let you get some rest. It was nice talking to you, Mateo," said Samantha.

"It was nice talking to you too, Samantha," said Mateo, as he lay back down on the bed, resting his head on a flat and hardened pillow.

He quietly drifted off to sleep while Samantha lay in the bed, staring up at the openings in the ceiling where she could see a couple stars dotting the night sky. She then shut her eyes and drifted off to sleep.

Chapter 10: Mr. Harkin's Chicken Farm

Samantha naturally woke up in the early hours of the morning. Light from the sun shined through the only glass pane window in the hut. It was warm and humid inside the hut in the summer months of Texas. There was a foul smell of body odor and urine inside the hut. Something that Samantha didn't smell last night, but now suddenly smelt it. She opened her eyes and leaned up, looking around the small space at the other beds, noticing that the other children were already up and out of the hut doing whatever it was that they did here on this farm. Samantha climbed out of bed, staggered over to the door and opened it revealing the property and large home that Mr. Harkin resided in.

Taking a step out of the hut, Samantha looked over to where the barns were and walked over to one. The closer that she got to the barn, the more she heard the chickens clucking inside. She approached barn door and opened it. Stepping inside, she looked down at five different rows, with cages aligning each side of the rows with chickens caged in close with one another. The sound of the chickens clucking was absolutely deafening. She walked down one of the rows and saw that most of the chickens were laying eggs in their tight confinements.

"Hey!" yelled a voice behind her.

Samantha turned around and looked behind her, seeing the Mexican boy walking towards her from where she had just come.

"Mateo!" she yelled back over the sounds of the chickens.

"How'd you sleep last night?" yelled Mateo.

"Fine! What's going on in here?" asked Samantha.

"Work! This is our worksite! Come, follow me!" said Mateo as he turned around and walked back towards the barn door.

Samantha followed him outside.

"Hey! Sorry, it gets loud in there," said Mateo.

"It's fine. What's going on in there?"

"Chickens. They lay eggs throughout the day. So our job is to collect the eggs. Feed the chickens. Clean out their cages. We work all the barns here in a day."

"Where do the eggs go?"

"To the storage shed on the end of the property. They're stored there and then picked up and taken to a factory that cleans them up, puts them in cartons, and sends them out to whoever the chicken man sells them to."

Mateo turned and walked around the barn towards the door of the next barn over.

"Sometimes we have to kill the chickens, too. They catch diseases, get hurt, or just get too old to produce eggs anymore, so the chicken man has us kill them and get rid of them."

"How many others are here working in the barns?"

"Fifty-two of us are working in the barns."

"Fifty-two? Where did they all come from?"

"Everyone's from Mexico," said Mateo as he opened the barn door.

Samantha followed close behind him inside the barn too. "Some were sold by their parents to the chicken man. Some were sold off the streets. Homeless children. Some said they came from an all-boys' orphanage in Mexico City.

In this barn, Samantha saw that there were several baby chicks. Some of the Mexican children poured feed into the feeding troughs in the cages. The cheeping sounds the chicks were making weren't nearly as loud as the adult egg-laying chickens.

"This is where the chicken man stores the baby chicks. These are the future egg layers, so they need special care throughout the day. Feed, water, and then a lot of cleanups to reduce infection and diseases."

Samantha watched as one boy was on his hands and knees, scraping up dried chicken feces from the floor in the corner of one cage. He used a putty knife as he wedged it under the feces and pried it up. Some pieces of feces were stuck firmly onto the floor, so that when he used force to pry them off the floor, they would hit him in the face. Sticking to his sweat-drenched face.

"How long is it until they are ready to lay?" asked Samantha.

"Some won't be ready for a while still. Some that are turning from that yellow color to brown and white, they'll be ready to start laying in the upcoming months," said Mateo. "Do you know if you are leaving this morning for California?"

"I don't know. I haven't seen both the men since they put me in the shed last night."

"If you can escape, then do it and get help. I don't have anything to give you to help out"

"I have a small pocketknife," said Samantha.

"Then, use it when the time is right. However, you need to use it. The last thing you want is to be sold off to someone. You're going to have to do something to help yourself out, and when you do, remember us here at this farm. I'm not sure how much longer I will be here before I'm sold off, but at least the others can get some help."

"Samantha!" yelled a voice from outside the barn.

"That's him," said Samantha as a chill ran up her back, causing the hairs on her neck to stand on end.

"It'll be okay. Just remember what I said. Don't be sold to anyone or else you're never coming home," said Mateo as he walked over to the door and opened it.

Samantha walked out of the barn and into the open. Carl was over by the fence at the home on the edge of the yard. He spotted her and called out to her again.

"Come in here for breakfast. Then we need to go," he yelled as he turned around and walked inside.

Samantha walked up to the house, passing child workers who were going from barn to barn. Some carried eggs. Some were covered in sweat, mud and chicken feces. Some carried buckets of chicken feed. She passed the last barn and approached the fence. Walking through an open space in the fence, she walked up to the back door of the home and opened it. Stepping inside, she could hear talking coming from a distance within the home. Following the sounds of the voices, Samantha walked through a washroom, then down a long hallway towards a large dinner table where Carl was sitting in a chair at the table along with Mr. Harkin.

There were a couple of women there sitting at the table that Samantha hadn't met the night before either. One older and one younger.

"Well, good morning, sunshine. You are looking real cute this morning. Going to make someone really happy real soon," said Mr. Harkin as he had stood up and walked over to her and caressed the side of her face with the back of his hand.

"Have some breakfast," said Carl as he pointed at the table.

There were plates of pancakes, French toast, scrambled eggs, sausage links, slices of ham, pastries and fruit on the table, along with pitchers of orange juice, milk, and water.

Samantha walked up to an empty place at the table and pulled out the chair. Sitting in the chair, she pulled herself towards the table and took the fork next to the plate and began to dish herself up breakfast.

"Bet you haven't eaten this good in a long time. Even when you were with your parents have you?" asked Mr. Harkin.

"We have breakfast at my house. Mom likes to make pancakes. I'm just really hungry. Haven't eaten since yesterday morning," replied Samantha as she reached out, grabbing a piece of bacon and stuffing it into her mouth.

"Is that true, Carl?"

"I was busy protecting her from a child rapist. Forgive me if I forgot to feed her," said Carl.

"That seems like a fair trade to me. Well, enjoy your breakfast this morning. You are my guest."

Samantha didn't respond to Mr. Harkin, only dished her plate until it was full.

"Do you like syrup?" asked Mr. Harkin.

"Yes, please," said Samantha.

"Of course." He said as he reached across the table and grabbed a small pitcher of maple syrup. He set it down in front of Samantha, who grabbed it and poured the syrup all over her food.

"Alright, Carl, so after breakfast you guys are taking off. I have a call this morning to one of the senators here in Texas. Guy named Boyd Masterson. He owes me a couple of favors, so I will talk with him over the phone and ask him to see about getting his hands on that cell phone of your friend you so effortlessly killed in a gas station bathroom. I'm sure either the highway patrol or the rangers are going to investigate it. I'm sure they've already found the body and I'm sure one of them have that god damn cell phone in evidence. Boyd can get it for me. In the meantime though, you have the keys for the brown car in the garage. Take that to California, and we'll deal with the van here."

Samantha started eating while Mr. Harkin and Carl were talking. She hadn't tasted food this good in a long time. While she was eating, the two women at the table watched her intently as she took each bite. She realized that they were watching her while she was in mid-bite. She stopped, then swallowed and looked over to Mr. Harkin.

"May I have some milk, please?" she asked.

"Of course, you can," he said, pouring her a glass of milk from the pitcher.

He pushed the glass in front of her, and Samantha took the glass and drank from it.

"So, are you ready for this Friday?" asked Mr. Harkin.

"What's this Friday?"

"The auction. I'd imagine you're going to make me a decent amount of money. You're gorgeous, honey. Curves in all the right places and at twelve years old. Girls like you should have curves like that for at least a couple more years."

Samantha was nervous and didn't respond. She lost her appetite after hearing Mr. Harkin say that. She pushed her plate of food away from her.

"Go ahead, eat up," said Mr. Harkin.

"I'm not hungry anymore," said Samantha.

"Oh, come now. Of course you are. I didn't mean anything by what I said. Just paying you a compliment. A lot of people may think I'm a bad person. I'm really not. Those kids out there, I give them a place to stay and to work. They have shelter and access to food. You should see the environment they come from. Parents who can't take care of them. Support them. Help them grow and be something. I give them that opportunity. An opportunity that they don't have in Mexico."

"And what happens when they grow older?"

"They go on and live productive lives wherever they go."

"It doesn't seem productive to me."

"Child. You don't know what it's really like in the world. You see, I give these children opportunities that they didn't have when they were with their families in Mexico. You don't have to worry about these things because you had parents who would take care of problems for you."

"So, it's a simple question. Where do they go when they become adults?"

"It's none of your concern where they go. Look, all your concern is to focus on this Friday evening. It's the beginning of a brand-new life for you! No matter what, you're going to be sold to someone who is rich beyond your wildest dreams. They can afford anything for you. You'll be taken care of for the rest of your life. How does that sound to you?"

"I want to go home."

"And home you soon will be, child. Your new home. A better home."

"There is no better home than with my mom and dad."

"Well, you can forget about them and focus on your new life," said Mr. Harkin, as he pushed his chair away from the table and stood up.

As soon as he did, his cell phone rang in his pocket. He walked into the kitchen, but with the open concept in the kitchen and dining room area, his conversation was easily heard. He put the call on speaker phone so that Carl could hear as well.

"Mr. Masterson," he said, answering the call.

"Mr. Harkin, it's a pleasure to hear from you again. How have you been?" replied Boyd Masterson, a senator from Texas.

"I've been doing well, Boyd. Thank you for asking."

"Did you hear about Trevor Richardson?"

"Trevor from college?"

"The same one. He died a few weeks back."

"Well, I'll be goddamned. How about that?" said Mr. Harkin. "How is his family doing?"

"They're fine. Holding up. His wife moved back to South Carolina to be closer to her side of the family. Took their two kids with them ."

"Well, I'll have to try to reach out to her and see how she's doing."

"How is Cynthia doing?"

"Oh, she's just fine. Sitting at the table right now. Say hi, Cynthia," he said, raising the phone up towards her at the table.

"Hi Boyd!' she yelled across the table to the phone.

"How are you doing, Cynthia?" asked Boyd.

"Things are going great," she replied.

"And your daughter?" asked Boyd.

"She's here too."

"Hi Jennifer!"

"Hi Boyd!"

"Going to college this fall still?"

"I am. To Yale."

"Good for you. I'm glad you picked Yale to go to. Great school there. I'll talk with the admissions counselor there. I'm sure we can get you in there and get your tuition paid in full, too."

"Thanks, Boyd!

"I appreciate that too, Boyd. I also need your help with something else that happened."

"Oh? What is it, Mr. Harkin?"

"I got a little situation. You know Carl, right?"

"Sure. I remember meeting him. He was doing some jobs for you."

"He was. Well, a little incident happened yesterday."

"What's that?"

"He had a friend that was working with him. Guy named Bo, I don't think you ever met him."

"Name doesn't sound familiar, no."

"Well, turns out he tried to rape the girl that they had picked up there in Miami," said Mr. Harkin.

"Jesus. Seriously?"

"Yeah, right there in a gas station bathroom. I knew the guy a little bit. He was always the kind of guy who thought with his dick instead of his goddamn stupid brain. Anyway, Carl broke into the bathroom there. Hit him in the back of the head a couple of times, then stomped the son of a bitch's head into a pancake, right there on the bathroom floor."

"Goddamn it, Carl. Nicely done. Never cared much for pedophiles."

"You and me neither. But the problem is that this fucker had his phone on him. Carl picked up his wallet and thought his phone was in the van. However, it was in his pocket. So I'm sure the police have the phone."

"You know what, I think I remember hearing about this. Where did it happen, Carl?" asked Boyd.

"Cove, Texas," said Carl.

"At Buckie's gas station, right?"

"Yes, sir. That's right."

"I read you. I did hear about that. Jesus Christ, Carl. You really did a number on that guy," said Boyd as he typed in the background. "Alright. Don't worry, Josh. Turns out the Texas Rangers are doing the lead for investigating. Which is good. I know their assistant chief really well. I can make a call and get this case shut down and get that phone destroyed, too. Don't worry about that at all."

"Boyd, I appreciate you. I'll send you a check in the mail for all your troubles," said Mr. Harkin.

"Well, that's awfully nice of you to do, Josh. Thank you. My wife and I are planning a fourteen-day cruise to the Caribbean. Leaving Galveston in a couple of months. We can use that money for our trip."

"That sounds great. Cynthia and I need to get out and do something like that," said Mr. Harkin.

"Yes, that does sound nice," said Mr. Harkins wife.

"So how is the girl from Miami?" asked Boyd.

"Fine. Doing much better now. She just had breakfast. She and Carl are going to be leaving here soon. I'm getting their van off the road for a bit. Probably going to drive it out into the desert and just incinerate it."

"Might not be a bad idea. Good to get rid of any and all evidence there, Josh. You selling this girl at the Wine and Dine?"

"Yeah, she's on her way to the house between Beverly Hills and Hollywood."

"You think you're going to get a lot for this one?"

"Not sure how much profit. I'm thinking low end, $50,000. The higher end $70,000."

"That's pretty good, Josh. Good money."

"It usually is. The kids I buy from Mexico help to supplement the farm here too."

"I see that. My wife and I buy your eggs in the store. We look for your brand name every time."

"Appreciate that, Boyd. Well, I need to get Carl and the girl out of here. They need to be at the Wine and Dine by Friday evening."

"Friday evening? They need to hurry up and get going then. It's about a day's drive to Hollywood, isn't it?"

"Close to that. Then they need time to clean her up, get her a dress that fits and shows some skin, and then display her for a little bit so the participants can see what they are bidding on."

"Well, I'll let you get to your business then. Don't worry about the Rangers. I'll handle that right now. You just worry about handling your business."

"Appreciate it, Boyd. Thank you. Let's get together soon for a vacation at the end of the summer."

"You and Cynthia should join us on the cruise."

"You know what, we may just do that," said Mr. Harkin.

"We're going to do that," yelled Cynthia from the table.

Everyone laughed, except Samantha.

"Have a good one, Josh."

"You too, Boyd. Bye now."

Mr. Harkin hung the phone up and stuffed it back into his pants pocket.

"You know what, we should go on a vacation. Carl, when you drop Samantha off here in the next couple days in California, why don't you come back and keep an eye on the farm for us. Make sure they keep working. You know, while the cat's away the mice will play kinda thing."

"You sign the checks, Mr. Harkin. I can be back here after I drop her off," said Carl.

"Good man. You got the keys to the car?"

"Yes, sir."

"Well, little girl, are you ready to get out of here and get on with the rest of your life?"

Samantha didn't say anything but pushed herself away from the table and stood up. She walked out the back door without making eye contact with anyone.

"I'll take that as a yes then," said Mr. Harkin.

"Don't worry, sir. I'll get her to Hollywood just fine," said Carl.

"I'm sure you will. Don't let me down, Carl."

"I won't, sir."

"Do you want some water bottles for the road, Carl?" asked Cynthia.

"Yes, please. I'll move the cooler from the van to the car, but if we could get some more water bottles, I'd appreciate that."

"Of course, let me grab you some from the fridge."

"Thank you, Mrs. Harkins," said Carl, as he turned around and walked out the back door, out to where the barns and garage were. Not far ahead of him was Samantha, walking slowly towards the garage door. Carl quickened his pace to catch up with her.

"Look, I'm sorry that things are the way that they are right now," said Carl as he walked next to Samantha.

"Let me go back to my home then."

"I can't let you do that. I need to get something out of this deal. All I need is money. I don't care about sex. Or drugs. Or anything else. That shit don't matter to me. That and Mr. Harkin won't let you just walk away without getting something in return either."

"Why do you need money? Why don't you do some other kind of work?"

"Because the money is good doing this," said Carl, opening the garage door for them.

"But you could be doing something else other than kidnapping girls."

"Like what?"

"You could manage a store. Or be a mailman."

"You know what, Samantha. I've thought about that sometimes. If things could have been different for me," said Carl, opening the van and reaching inside to grab the cooler from between the front seats. "What if I'd stuck it out in school? Finished high school. Went to college. I'm not like other people, for whom that shit comes easy. I never had a chance of growing up to have a life like that. So I guess here I am."

"But you could make things right. Taking kids away from their mom and dad isn't a nice thing to do."

"Neither was getting your ass beat by your drunk dad, or missing in action mom growing up too, but these are the cards we're dealt in life that we have to play with," said Carl, as he opened the back door of a gold Toyota Camry car, stuffing the ice cooler into the back seat.

"So, make things right now then," said Samantha.

"There is no more time to make things right in my life, Samantha," replied Carl as he opened the passenger door to the car.

"There's always time," she replied as she got in and sat in the passenger seat.

Carl shut the door behind her and stopped for a minute, thinking to himself before he got into the driver's side and started the car. He backed out of the garage and pulled up to the back door of the house where Mrs. Harkin was waiting with a plastic shopping bag full of water bottles in hand. Carl pulled up by her, rolling Samantha's passenger side window down.

"The cooler is in the back seat," said Carl.

"Okay, I'll put them in there. I filled up the bag with some ice to help keep them cool for you too," said Cynthia.

"Thank you, Mrs. Harkin."

Mr. Harkin walked out the back door and met them both at the passenger window. Putting both hands on the door, he leaned down.

"Alright, you two, stay safe. Carl, when you finish up with his job, come back to the farm," said Mr. Harkin.

"Sure, I can do that, sir."

Mr. Harkin reached through the passenger window, handing Carl a folded piece of paper.

"What's this?" asked Carl.

"Address in Santa Ana, California. Take you to church. Let the reverend know that I sent you and show him the girl. He'll know what to do."

Mr. Harkin looked down at Samantha, who was sitting quietly in the passenger seat.

"And you, little girl. It was a pleasure meeting you. You take care of yourself too."

Samantha didn't reply to him.

Mr. Harkin smiled, tapped the door twice with his right hand and then let go of the passenger door. Carl drove off and down the driveway, passing the barns and farm and some of the children who were there working for free. Samantha looked up and out the passenger window where she saw Mateo, walking along the side of the road back towards the worker shacks. He turned, made eye contact with her, smiled, raised his arm and waved to Samantha.

It was the last time they would ever see one another. Samantha waved back, but couldn't muster up the strength to smile. Soon, the farm was long gone in the rearview, and they were pulling onto the interstate, continuing their journey west to Hollywood.

Chapter 11: Tucson, Arizona

The blazing heat of the midday sun made the ground look hazy as Carl drove west to Las Cruces. The humidity made it even more uncomfortable. Driving to Las Cruces, New Mexico, and then to Tucson, Arizona did not make it any cooler of a drive. Fortunately for Carl and Samantha, the car had air conditioning, which ran throughout the drive. At times, Carl turned the air conditioning off before the engine in the car overheated. Which made the drive even more miserable for Samantha, who was sitting in the passenger seat, staring out the window into the desert.

"You want to listen to some music?" asked Carl as he looked over at Samantha.

"I don't care," she replied, keeping her gaze out the window.

"Sometimes on long drives like this, it's nice to have something to listen to. What's your favorite music group?"

"Matchbox Twenty."

"Seriously? You hear that from your dad?" Carl laughed.

"You asked. I answered," said Samantha.

"Okay, okay. I'm sorry. I don't know if I can manage that, but I can try to find some 80s and 90s music. That's pretty close to Matchbox Twenty," said Carl as he leaned over and turned the radio on, switching through the channels as the speakers crackled, followed by someone on a talk show or Spanish music.

"You sure you don't like Mexican music?" asked Carl.

"I don't even like Mexican food," said Samantha.

"Yeah, I hear you there. The food's too spicy for me. Can't handle anything hotter than mild salsa."

Carl finally found a radio station that he assumed that Samantha would like to listen to. He left the radio dial on the station as it cut in and out of reception.

"There. It's not the greatest, but at least you can understand what they're saying," said Carl.

Samantha didn't respond.

Carl continued driving, scanning the desert horizon in both directions. He saw nothing but cactus and sagebrush for miles.

"Did you know that there are spiders the size of your face out there in that desert, just wandering around and living their lives?" asked Carl.

"I don't care," said Samantha, keeping her gaze out the window.

"Now, Samantha, you and I are going to be together for a couple more days. Can't you just get along with me for 48 more hours?"

Samantha didn't respond.

Carl cleared his throat and sat back in the driver's seat before he started speaking again.

"I often wonder what it would be like to live a normal life," said Carl.

Samantha turned to look at Carl, who kept his gaze straight ahead to the road.

"What if I had done better in school, you know? Tried harder."

"Why didn't you?" Asked Samantha.

"When I was six years old, my mom died. Breast cancer. Doctors didn't catch it in time, so they tried chemotherapy, but the cancer had already spread from the tissue to the bone. It was only a matter of time. In about a month of chemo, she died. Just went to bed one night and never woke up again. It fucked with my dad's mind. Mine too. The night of the funeral, after they put her body in the ground, he started drinking. Drinking led to coke. Coke led to dealing the powder and making money on the side. Throughout this whole time, he got abusive to me. Physically. Verbally. No matter how good I did with my grades or in school performance, he never gave a shit. Got me so pissed off that I ran away from home when I was seventeen. Met Mr. Harkin through a friend of mine, who gave me a job working on his farm, and in no time I was doing jobs for him. And not cleaning chicken shit from the cages or dispatching sick chickens from the roost either. I started picking up girls for him over twenty years ago, and he's taken good care of me ever since."

"Why are you telling me this?"

"You know what, I don't know. I've never told anyone that before in my life. I guess I feel comfortable enough around you to be brutally honest. Feels like you might understand me a little better."

"Why didn't you just let it happen?"

"Let what happen?"

"Back in the bathroom at the gas station. Why didn't you just let your friend do what he wanted with me? Was it really about the money?" asked Samantha.

"Part of it is about the money, yes?"

"And what's the other part?"

"That you remind me of my daughter."

"Your daughter? I thought your friend Bo was the only one that had a daughter?"

"No. I had a girlfriend about ten years ago. We had a baby girl together. Our relationship lasted for about eight years then she got suspicious about the work I did. I wouldn't tell her what I did, and she thought that was weird. We got into a fight about it one evening, and she took our daughter and moved away."

"Where did they move to?"

"Seattle, up in Washington state. She had family there."

"When was the last time you saw your daughter?"

"Just before she left about ten years ago. This year she will turn eighteen. But I see a lot of her in you. From the color of your hair to the attitude you give me and how you talk to me, even the way you eat your fries and food. It's just uncanny."

"So, would you be okay doing this to your daughter?"

Carl, for the first time, thought about his answer before giving it to Samantha.

"No. I wouldn't."

"So why are you forcing me into this?"

"Well, I need to realize that you are not my daughter. I'm sorry, but you're not. But goddamn it's hard to get it out of my mind. It really is. Maybe when I'm finished here, I'll head north to Seattle instead of going back to the farm and try to find her again."

"Why don't you just go find her now?"

"I can't. I have work to do first. Making sure you make it safe to Los Angeles so that you get to the auction. But before we go there, we need to make a stop."

"A stop? Where?"

"Santa Ana."

"To church?"

"That's right. Mr. Harkin knows the reverend of the church there. He helps clean the girls up before they go to the Wine and Dine."

"How far of a drive is it to Santa Ana?" asked Samantha.

"Have you ever been out west before?"

"No."

"Oh. Well, from here it's about another twelve hours to get to Santa Ana, in California. The next town we're coming up to is Las Cruces. Then we'll connect to Interstate 10 and head west."

"How far away is Las Cruces?"

"Not far. Maybe an hour. We'll stop in Tucson for lunch."

"Tucson?"

"In Arizona."

"How far away is that?"

"From where we are? Probably like four hours."

Samantha got more and more worried the further she traveled west. All the towns that she was passing through and that Carl was talking about were foreign to her. She didn't recognize anything or know anyone out this way. Staring out the window, she saw businesses and buildings that she didn't recognize after having lived in Illinois her whole life.

"Are you tired?" asked Carl.

"What?"

"Did you sleep okay last night?"

"I guess. It was hot in the shack. Hard to stay cool and rest comfortably."

"Well, why don't you take a nap, and I'll wake you up when we reach Tucson."

"I'm not sleepy."

"If you tried, you might surprise yourself. It's fine. Lean the seat back and try to get some rest."

Samantha did just that. She reached down to the side of the seat and pulled the lever, leaning the backrest back. She lay back and closed her eyes, and before she knew it, she was fast asleep.

*   *   *   *

Samantha woke up with the sun pouring down into the cabin of the car. She leaned up and looked around her, seeing the same thing that she had seen before. Desert. Cactus. Large rocks. Heat hit the asphalt, causing a mirage to dance off the road. She looked over and saw Carl was still driving, eyes forward.

"What time is it?" asked Samantha as she raised her backrest up to an upright position.

"2:00 PM," said Carl.

"How much further to Tucson?"

"Not much further at all. Probably ten minutes."

"I'm hungry."

"Yeah, so am I. We'll hit a drive-thru somewhere in Tucson and grab some food. You thirsty too?"

"Yes."

"Reach into the cooler and grab yourself a water."

"I need to go to the bathroom too," she said as she grabbed herself a water from the cooler.

"Jesus Christ. Are you serious? We just passed a goddamn rest stop fifteen minutes ago."

"I'm sorry."

"It's fine. Well, just go inside the restaurant instead of the drive-thru. I need to get up and walk around, anyway."

"Where are you looking to eat?"

"At this point I really don't care. Food. Can be burgers. Can be Mexican. Hell, it could even be Chinese. I don't care at this point."

Tucson came into full view as they drove through the suburbs in the southeast corner of the city, passing the Rita Ranch area and Little Town. Finally, they came into South Tucson, where they promptly found a local fast-food restaurant to stop at.

"Here. This will do," said Carl, as he slowed the car down and pulled into the parking lot.

"That's fine," said Samantha.

Carl pulled into the parking lot and parked the car near the doors of the establishment.

"Alright, listen. Don't give me any trouble here, you understand. Don't fuck this up for me, or else it may not go well with your parents back home. I will go to their home and kill them while they sleep. So, if you don't want that to happen, then you will behave. Got it?"

"Yeah."

"Don't talk to anyone in there either. You've got no business talking with anyone."

"I understand."

Carl reached over and unlocked the seatbelt from the passenger seat.

"Alright. Get out."

"I'm going to use the bathroom first in there," said Samantha as she opened the door and stepped outside.

"That's fine. I'll order for us. What do you want?" asked Carl as he too got out of the driver's seat and stretched his legs for the first time since leaving Sonora, Texas.

"Chicken nuggets."

"Fine. You want sauce?"

"Sweet and sour."

"Great. Come to a burger fast-food restaurant, end up getting fucking chicken," said Carl as he walked around the front of the car, grabbing Samantha by the arm as she waited there for him.

They walked into the restaurant together. He nudged her along into the lobby of the restaurant. Inside there were a couple of families eating, while their children played in the toy room with the slides and the ball pit. Samantha paused for a moment there in the lobby to watch the kids playing without a care in the world. They were no older than five or six years old. The oldest may have been seven years old. Carl walked up behind her and grabbed Samantha by the shoulder, turning her around to walk up to the counter.

"Forget playing with those kids. Order what you want and let's get going," said Carl as he nudged Samantha towards the counter.

Soon, one of the workers came from the back area to the front counter and spoke with them.

"Sorry about that. It's just me and two other guys here today. More than half our crew called in sick or didn't show up to work today," said the young man, who looked as if he had just graduated high school yesterday.

"It's fine. What do you want?" Carl asked Samantha as he glared down at her.

She looked up at the menu on the wall behind the worker and found what she wanted.

"Chicken nuggets."

"Ten or twenty pieces?" asked the worker.

"Ten please," she replied.

"You want the meal?"

"Yes."

"With fries, tater tots, onion rings?"

"Onion rings."

The young man reached down and pulled out a drinking cup and handed it to Samantha, who promptly took it from him and walked over to the soda fountain.

"And for you, sir?" he asked Carl.

"Number four, please."

"Deluxe bacon cheeseburger. Everything on it?"

"Sure."

"Fries, tater tots, onion rings?"

"Fries."

"Anything else?" asked the worker.

"No, that's it," said Carl, as he looked over to where Samantha was pouring ice into her cup and selecting root beer from the fountain.

"Alright, for the two meals, medium size, that'll be twenty-six dollars and fifty-two cents."

"You can keep the change," Carl said as he paid in cash and grabbed his cup.

"Thanks, sir. Here's your receipt. Order number eighty-two."

"Thanks," said Carl as he took the receipt and walked towards Samantha, who had just finished pouring her root beer into her cup. Carl poured ice into his cup, then filled it with orange soda.

"You drink orange soda too?" asked Samantha.

"Yes, why?"

"My dad drinks orange soda. I've always been the root beer drinker in my family."

"Well, maybe your husband will drink orange soda, too. Who knows? Find a seat here in the lobby. We'll eat here."

"I thought we were taking it to go?"

"No, were not going to eat in the car. Find a table in here," said Carl.

Samantha walked over to the back corner of the lobby, next to the window. There she found a quiet table where she sat down. Carl sat across from her. Both took drinks from their cups and set them down on the table.

"I need to use the bathroom," said Samantha.

"Goddamn you are about as bad as a cocker spaniel," whispered Carl, making sure no one heard him. "Go ahead and go. Be back here in five minutes. If you're not back in five minutes, I'm coming into that bathroom."

"Okay," said Samantha, as she slid out from the bench seat and walked through the lobby to the front door of the restaurant.

She passed through the door and walked into the women's restroom. Walking up to the sink and the mirror, she paused for a moment and stood there, looking at herself in the reflection when she got an idea.

Samantha turned and walked out of the women's restroom. She leaned against the wall, out of Carl's sight. She looked around the corner, out into the lobby and saw Carl sitting there at the table. He was looking down at his cell phone, not paying attention to the lobby area.

"Order number eighty-two!" yelled the worker behind the counter.

Carl stood up from the table and walked to the front counter, where Samantha could hear Carl and the worker speaking for just a moment.

"You want ketchup packets with that?"

"Sure," he replied.

"Anything else?"

"Hell, I don't know. Ranch. Sweet and sour? Barbecue? Just give me one of every dip, and she can figure out what she wants when she's back out here."

The worker put one of each dip on the food tray, and Carl thanked the young man, then turned around and walked back towards the table. While walking back to the table, he heard a ding at the door to the restaurant, indicating that someone had come in or someone had left.

He turned around and looked to see if someone had come in, but no one new had just walked into the restaurant lobby.

Samantha ran around the corner of the building, and into the parking lot of a shopping mall that was next door to the restaurant. She ran toward the mall's entrance when she turned around and saw Carl run out of the restaurant and spot her. He dashed after her while she sprinted for the mall, but it was too far away. Samantha quickly ducked between the cars to her left and hid between them. Ducking down, she moved around the cars, hoping that they would keep her hidden.

Carl ran into the mall parking lot and stopped for a moment. Samantha stopped as well. She sat between the fronts of two vehicles, propping her back up against the front of one as she heard his footsteps come to a stop nearby. Samantha lowered herself to the ground and crawled under the car she was hiding behind. Looking up, she saw Carl's shoes pacing toward the back of the car she was under.

Samantha held her breath and stayed as still as she could as she watched Carl's shoes shuffle between the cars on the passenger side of the vehicle, slowly as if he was waiting to hear or see her move somewhere. She quietly drew her legs under the car to now completely be hidden under the vehicle, as Carl had just reached the front of the car. He looked down between the front of both vehicles then stopped and stood in place. Samantha watched as his feet walked away between the vehicles and to a different part of the parking lot.

Samantha lay still for a moment when she felt that it was clear to get out from underneath the car and continue to run away. She worked her way to the back of the vehicle when she crawled out and stood up. Looking around, she turned to her left and made eye contact with Carl, who was a couple of aisles away.

She bolted, running in the opposite as he gave chase. Running between more vehicles, she ducked and did her best to hide again as Carl drew closer, but he was faster, and Samantha couldn't get under a car in time. All she could do was hide between the cars, next to a white minivan. She sat down between two vehicles, propping her back up against the driver's side door as Carl ran up to the same van, but on the passenger side of the van.

Hearing his footsteps come to a complete stop, she held her breath as he circled the back of the van, heading right towards her. Carl was a few steps away from finding her when the van beeped a couple of times and unlocked, startling both her and Carl. He stopped and turned around to see a family approaching the van that she was hiding next to. A mom with three of her children. All of them carried bags of clothing with them.

"Oh, hello," said Carl to the woman.

"Hi," said the woman, a little apprehensive that a strange man she didn't know was talking to her in the parking lot. "Can I help you?"

"Oh, no. No, I was just looking for a ring that I had dropped around here. I was hoping that I could find it, but I dropped it around here about an hour ago."

"Oh. Well, I'm sorry to hear that. I hope you find what you're looking for," said the woman as she opened the side of the minivan and ushered her kids inside.

"Thanks. Went shopping today?" asked Carl.

"Yeah. Getting a head start on school shopping," said the woman as the last kid jumped into the minivan.

"School already. I'm Carl, by the way."

"Have a nice day," she said as she shut the van door and walked around the side to the driver's side door.

She got into the van and started it, then backed out of the parking stall. Carl stood there watching until she was gone, but nothing was there. He walked away, between the cars, as Samantha watched him from underneath the car that was parked next to the van. She started crawling out from under the vehicle when the car above her started. The vehicle startled her, and she hurried her pace, crawling out from under the car as the wheels started turning.

The oblivious driver spoke on their phone as Samantha crawled as fast as she could, barely swinging her legs out from under the vehicle before the front tire could back over them. The driver was still oblivious to the fact that he had nearly run over a young girl as the conversation he was having on the phone with his wife was more engaging than paying attention to what was going on around him. When the car had completely backed out, he shifted into gear and took off. Samantha started to run again when she felt a hand grab the back of her hair and tighten. She let out a yelp and turned around to see that Carl had grabbed her by the hair.

"You goddamn little bitch! What the fuck do you think you are doing?" he said with anger in his eyes.

Samantha was deathly afraid when Carl grabbed her by the arm tightly and walked her out of the mall parking lot back towards the car at the restaurant they had originally been at. He unlocked the vehicle and shoved her into the passenger seat.

"Goddamn you, kid, why do you have to fuck around with me like that?" he said as he violently strapped her into the passenger seat with the seatbelt. "I swear to God, if you weren't worth some money, I would beat the fuck out of you myself!"

Carl slammed the passenger door, got into the driver's side and backed out of the parking lot quickly, tires squealing.

A woman in a white van who had just completed school shopping early for her children was stopped nearby the restaurant to take a call on her cell phone. She had seen everything that had transpired and called 911.

Chapter 12: Santa Ana, California

"Alright ma'am, so I just want to repeat back what I had heard you say," said the Tucson police officer, taking a report of what the woman in the white minivan had seen.

"A man dressed in a black shirt with blue jeans. Middle aged. Balding. Had a brown beard. Wearing bifocals. He grabbed this younger girl that looked to be in her early teens. She had dark brown hair that hung low to the center of her back. He forcefully walked her out of the mall parking lot next door. Then he walked her back to this vehicle parked here at the restaurant, yes?"

"Yes, that's right," said the woman, who was sitting in the van with the driver's window down.

"What kind of car was it?"

"I don't know, like a four-door gold-colored car," said the woman.

"Did you get a license plate number?" asked the officer.

"No. I didn't in time before it had pulled out and onto the road. But I could see it was from Texas. It had the three letters of BLW at the beginning."

"Texas plates and letters BLW?"

"Yes, sir."

"Which direction was the vehicle heading, ma'am?"

"It turned out of the lot and went right, so I'm guessing north."

"So, after the vehicle pulled out of the parking lot, did you follow and come back here? Or what did you do?"

"No, I stayed here and called 911. It just looked wrong. Like it wasn't his kid. He didn't handle her as if she were his. The way he grabbed her hair, and then her arm, and shoved her into the passenger seat of the car. Something was different. I don't think it was her parents."

"I see."

"What are you going to do?" asked the woman.

"Not really sure what can be done here, ma'am. You're trying to find a needle in a haystack out here in Tucson. Texas isn't too far away, so maybe they went back? Maybe they didn't. Who knows? Especially with them having left almost a full hour ago, who knows where they could have gone, or even if they left town?"

"You're going to do something though, right? I seriously think something was wrong. Like that girl was kidnapped."

"Of course we'll try, ma'am. I'm just not sure whether we're going to find anything. But we will certainly try and put a call out here in the area to look for a gold four-door sedan with Texas state license plates. We appreciate your information."

She smiled and thanked the officer as she rolled up her windows and drove away. The officer walked back to his patrol vehicle, where his partner was waiting for him in the passenger seat, writing a report on the laptop in the car. The officer opened the driver's side door and sat inside.

"Get what you needed?" asked the officer in the passenger seat.

"Goddamn it is hot as hell out there." He sighed, looking down at his notes.

"Yeah, I think I did. Sounds like a kidnapping, maybe? But no parents are reporting that their kid was kidnapped. All we have is a gold-colored four-door sedan. Maybe a Toyota Camry. Texas state plates that start with BLW."

"Maybe the man was the kid's dad?"

"Maybe."

"You want to check other jurisdictions and see if there are any reports of a kidnapping?"

"I don't know. Seems like a lot of work for potentially nothing. Maybe it was a dad whose kid pissed him off, and he just overreacted in how he grabbed her and brought her back to the car."

"Still, in that case, it would warrant a call to family services, would it not?"

"You done with the laptop?" asked the officer in the driver's seat. "I need to write my notes into the database."

"Yeah, let me finish this last paragraph, and you can have it. You want something to eat from the restaurant here? They got good chicken sandwiches."

"Nah, I'm not hungry."

"So, what are you going to do with it?"

"Write up an informational report. See if something comes up in the future and then we can at least have the information in our system."

"Sure. I suppose."

"What would you do?"

"I'd check the database and see if there are any reports of missing children."

"And then?"

"And then check other agencies. FBI. Highway patrol. Even neighboring states too. Like California. New Mexico. Utah. Hell, even Texas. You never know, man. What if there is more to it than meets the eye? You yourself said the plates were from Texas, and you got a partial plate number. You could do something with that."

"Jesus, just seems like a lot of work for nothing."

"You won't know until you try," said the officer sitting in the passenger seat.

He pivoted the laptop on its swivel over to the officer in the driver's seat.

"Goddamn it. Alright. Go grab me a couple of those chicken burgers. Fries. Fry sauce. Cola to drink."

"All of a sudden hungry?"

"No. Just going to be here for a while checking all these god damn systems, so I may as well have a late lunch as it is."

*   *   *   *

Carl continued driving nonstop to Santa Ana, California. He drove north to Phoenix, then stayed on Interstate 10 as he headed west and into the state of California. The heat was unbearable in this part of the state as they approached the Joshua Tree National Park area. Carl kept silent for the entire drive and so did Samantha, who only stared out the passenger window. With Mt. San Jacinto to the left and an endless expanse of desert to the right, Samantha watched as they passed windmills, sagebrush, power lines, and dry, desert sands. She paused for a moment and looked over at Carl.

"Where are we going?" she asked.

"Santa Ana."

"How much further?"

"Hour and a half."

"Can we stop for a bit?"

"Fuck no."

"You hurt my arm," she said, pulling her sleeve back and revealing handprint bruise.

"I don't give a shit, to be honest with you. I told you not to fuck around with me and what did you do? You try to run away from me. After I bought you lunch and everything. I'm so goddamn sick and tired of people running away from me," said Carl with frustration in his voice.

"I'm sorry," said Samantha.

"I don't care."

"What do you mean, people running away from you?"

"My wife and daughter ran away from me is what I mean."

"So?"

"It pisses me off."

"Why? I'm not your daughter."

"I didn't say you were."

"Then why are you treating me like your daughter?"

"I'm not."

"Then why get so mad?"

"Because that's my goddamn paycheck."

"Bullshit."

"Watch your mouth, Jennifer!"

Silence hung in the car. Samantha broke it moments later with a question.

"Who's Jennifer?"

"Shut up. It was the last kid I drove out here is all."

"It's your daughter's name, isn't it?"

There was a deafening silence in the car as Carl didn't answer her question. However, Samantha was persistent.

"It was her name, wasn't it?" she asked with intent.

"It was."

"I'm not your daughter."

"I know. Don't worry, I know."

"So why treat me like it?"

"I don't know. Just sit there, shut up, and let me get to Santa Ana."

"Why are you treating me like your daughter?"

"Because maybe I was robbed of her childhood, alright? Fuck, what is it with you and the questions?"

"You were robbed of her childhood. But I'm not your daughter. And treating me like your daughter is not going to bring her back. You grab her that hard, too?"

"I did. Once."

"When?"

"Just before my ex took off with my daughter to Seattle."

Before Samantha could ask another question, Carl cut her off before she could ask.

"I wasn't abusive to my daughter."

"I didn't say you were, but it's weird to me that you would lose your temper and grab me that hard."

"You pissed me off. That was a waste of time. Effort. Food. And you ask me why I lost my temper?"

"Yes. I do," she said, making stern eye contact with him. "And your ex and daughter left for Seattle shortly after you were physical with her like you were with me. Have you hurt them before?"

"I would never harm a hair on my daughter's head. It was that bitch I was with."

"What do you mean?"

"She made accusations about me, none of which were true."

There was silence in the car for a moment again. The sound of cars passing them could be heard, along with other common road noise.

"I did hurt her once, okay? But it was an accident. Absolutely unintentional accident."

"What happened?" Asked Samantha.

"I was out in the garage. Working on fixing the push lawnmower on a Saturday. I asked her to hold a flashlight for me as I was unscrewing a bolt from under the mower. She kept moving it around, and she was making it hard to do what I had to do, so I grabbed the light from her, held it myself while I unscrewed the light, and then I threw the light out from under the mower. And I hit her in the eye. Yeah, I was upset and frustrated. But in no way did I intend to hit her like that. Her mother never forgave me for that. Never let me forget it, too. Practically every time we had an argument, it would get brought up."

"Is that the only time something like that happened?" asked Samantha.

"Yes. On top of that, I had a couple beers that afternoon, so honestly I wasn't in the right frame of mind, anyway. But that was the last time I had had anything to drink too, and the last time that I had ever lost my temper with my daughter."

Samantha was skeptical of Carl's story. It didn't make sense that his girlfriend would take their daughter and move to the northwestern part of the country and away from him for something that was really just an accident. Especially after what she had witnessed him killing Bo back gas station bathroom and how hard he had handled her recently, too. He was hiding something.

They passed a sign on the freeway that welcomed them to Santa Ana, California. Entering the city limits, Carl slowed the vehicle down and took the exit from the freeway into the Tustin area of Santa Ana.

"Alright. From here I need Red Hill Avenue," he said.

Samantha didn't reply as she was certain that he wasn't asking her for directions. Not only had she never been here before, but she also knew nothing about driving, outside of what she saw from her mom and dad.

"Briggs. It's supposed to be down Briggs Avenue. Just off Red Hill," said Carl as he turned down Briggs Avenue, looking to his left.

"There it is. Holy Family Catholic Church," said Carl, as he parked along the side of the street in front of the large cathedral church doors.

"Why are we here?" asked Samantha.

"Because you need to get cleaned up. Get a shower. Get clothes that are attractive, and then we need to get going to Los Angeles."

"And the pastor here is supposed to do that?"

"The priest here, has been working for Mr. Harkin for years now," said Carl as he turned off the vehicle and unbuckled his seatbelt.

"Eight years, to be exact. I bring them here if the girl needs to be dressed sexier and cleaned up. He'll fix you up. And then we'll take off and go straight to the auction house in Los Angeles."

Carl got out of the car, opened the passenger side door and dragged Samantha out. He shut the door behind her, and they approached the church's solid wooden front doors adorned with large brass handles. Carl reached out and grabbed the lever and opened the door. They both walked into the church's narthex, where folding tables with fliers and brochures about the Catholic Church and Bible devotionals were spread out on them. Artwork depicting Jesus Christ hung on the walls. His crucifixion. Birth in Bethlehem. Preaching to the five thousand on a green hillside. Another painting depicted Jesus with his disciples out on the Sea of Galilee in a storm. The narthex was covered in a dim orange light, flickering as if meant to emulate a torch.

"Come on," said Carl as he dragged Samantha from the church's narthex into the nave of the church.

With each footstep, loud thumps reverberated throughout the church. They walked up to the chancel of the church, nearly reaching the sanctuary and altar when they heard a voice coming from their left.

"It has been a hot minute since we have seen one another, Carl," said the voice.

Samantha looked over, where she saw an older man stepping out of a room along the side of the chancel. Dressed in black slacks, he wore a short-sleeve black shirt and a white clerical collar around his neck. He was short and portly with a receding hairline and an old, worn tattoo of a seagull on the back of his hand. He stepped out into the sanctuary and stood up by the altar, looking at them both as they walked up.

"Good afternoon, priest," said Carl as he dragged Samantha towards the altar.

"Please call me Nixson. And what do we have here? Another fitting sacrifice?"

"Something like that, you could say," replied Carl as he stepped face to face with the priest, Samantha by his side as he gripped her arm tight.

"What is your name, my child?" said Nixson, stepping up and caressing the side of her face.

"Samantha," she said, backing away from the old man.

"What a beautiful name. I have a niece named Samantha. She went to USC here in Southern California. She graduated not that long ago. So what do you look to do with this one?"

"Mr. Harkin looks to sell this one up at the Wine and Dine house," said Carl.

"Up in Los Angeles. A good idea. The folks in that district would pay a pretty price for a young girl like this."

"That's what Mr. Harkin thinks as well."

"Where did she come from?"

"Chicago. Picked her up on her family trip in Florida and drove her to the chicken farm in Texas. Mr. Harkin told us to come here and that you would get her cleaned up and ready to go for the auction tonight."

"Mr. Harkin," said Nixson, laughing to himself. "What a scoundrel! Well, I would be happy to get her cleaned up for the auction tonight. Of course, for a nominal donation to the church."

"You mean your wallet, Reverend?" asked Carl.

"Indeed, the church." The old minister smiled as he turned and walked back towards the small room along the side of the chancel.

Carl dragged Samantha over towards the small room, and both went inside after Nixson. There was a desk and a bookshelf behind it in the small office. Windows offered a street view as cars passed by one after the other. The walls were old-fashioned wood stained and not painted over, and the room was a mess. Random objects and religious artifacts were scattered on shelves throughout the office.

"If you can forgive me for the mess in here. It's difficult to keep up the charade of actually being a real-life pastor. It's served me well over the years in making a profit for myself one way or the other," said Nixson.

"Priest," replied Carl.

"What?"

"You're a priest. Catholics have priests. Or reverends even. A pastor is someone from a Lutheran or a Baptist church."

"Well, whatever," said Nixson as he leaned down and retrieved some boxes from underneath his desk and opened the first one.

"Well, what size clothes do you think she is, Carl?"

"Size ten."

"Ten. Got it. What color dress do you think she should wear?"

"For the auction? Probably black. But a darker color would be appropriate."

"How about red?" asked Nixson.

"I don't like red," said Samantha.

"Red is good," replied Carl.

"Yes, here it is," said Nixson as he pulled out a red dress and held it up in front of her.

"Her little breasts would pop out in that, I may actually bid on her myself," said Nixson, as he set the dress down on the desk there in the office. "Now, what do you want her to smell like?"

"Smell?"

He opened the second box, revealing a variety of different labeled perfumes.

"Oh. I guess I never gave that much thought. What do you think?"

"I imagine either a vanilla scent or even a cherry vanilla would please the guests."

"Sure, that sounds good," said Carl.

"How about I give you both scent samplers and you can decide when you get there?"

"Fine by me."

"What scrub do you want me to use on her?"

"Scrub?"

"Body wash. She will need to take a bath, will she not?"

"It has been a while since she has been cleaned."

"So do you have a preference of body scrub?"

"No, I don't care. Just as long as the dirt and body odor are off her."

"Fine by me. I'll use a vanilla scrub," said Nixson, as he rummaged through the box.

He pulled out a bottle, along with a coarse sponge, from the box. He turned around and looked at her, a cracked smile on his face.

"Alright, my daughter. Come with me," said Nixson, as Carl walked away and sat in a chair by the door of the room.

"I'm not going with you anywhere. And if you want me to clean, then you're going to let me clean myself."

"I'm sorry, but it doesn't work that way. You won't clean yourself as much as you need to be scrubbed without my help. You know, the hard-to-reach places. I suggest you come with me so that I can help you," said Nixson.

"It's not going to happen."

Carl grabbed Samantha by the arm and walked her through another set of doors on the opposite end of the office, into a small bathroom. Nixson picked up some of the bathing supplies and brought them into the bathroom with them. A small bathtub sat next to a toilet, where Nixson turned the hot and cold faucets on and drew some water into the tub. Carl pushed Samantha into the room by the arm, shutting the door behind her and Nixson. Nixson proceeded to try to remove her shirt to prepare her for the bath when Samantha backed away from him again.

"You are not going to bathe me," she said in a loud voice.

"I don't give a shit what you want. It's not about you at this point. Stop making it about yourself and get into the tub."

"I don't want you to touch me!"

"I don't care!" said Nixson as he grabbed Samantha, fully clothed, and set her down into the bathtub forcefully.

"You will take a fuckin bath whether you like it or not, now get the fuck in there!"

Samantha landed in the tub with her legs and back first. The hot water soaked into her clothes and drenched her body. Her beautiful brown hair was soaked with bathwater.

"Take your shirt off," said Nixson, as he grabbed the sponge nearby and soaked it in the water.

Samantha, with no other choice, removed her shirt and curled it up into a ball and sat in the middle of the tub, hugging herself. Nixson took the sponge and squirted vanilla-scented body wash onto it. With his left hand, he pushed her head down, revealing her back as he took the sponge and violently scrubbed her skin. Each swipe of the sponge painfully scratched her back.

"You're hurting me," said Samantha.

"We need to dig deep into the skin. So it's going to hurt. I'll even do you a favor and let you keep your bra on."

Samantha was scared and cried as he continued to scrub the upper half of her body. She quietly disengaged from the reality around her and began to think of better times with her friends at school. Back home, having sleepovers with her closest childhood friend. Her parents and going on summer trips. Holidays with the family and get togethers. She felt absolutely helpless throughout this whole ordeal, accepting her fate to avoid any more hurt or pain, tolerant of what was happening to her in the moment. A strange man with his hands on her in a bathtub.

Nixson continued to scrub her all over her body. Her neck, back, chest. Removing her pants, he scrubbed her legs, feet, and buttocks as well. Nixson took her clothes, folded them neatly and set them on the countertop there next to the sink.

Samantha's only reprieve in the moment was that she didn't have to remove her underwear. Finally, he shampooed and conditioned her hair, using freshly drawn water from the faucet and a pitcher to pour fresh water to wash the soap out of her hair.

"Well, I see that you're not growing pubic hair yet either, so we won't have to shave. That's a good thing for you," said Nixson, as he was trying to speak positively about her. "Means that you will probably sell for more money in the auction."

Samantha didn't reply to him, sitting there in soapy, dirty water, holding her knees to her chest, covering herself with her own limbs.

"Let me get you a towel from the cabinet here," said Nixson as he stood up from beside the tub.

He leaned over and opened the cabinet and grabbed a purple body towel from it. He came back over to the edge of the tub.

"Stand up," he said.

Samantha complied.

Nixson wrapped the towel around her body. He then stood up and grabbed another towel from the cabinet and used it to dry her hair.

"Dry yourself off. I shouldn't have to help you dry off," he said as he helped to dry her hair.

Samantha took the towel and dried herself off while doing her best to stay covered up at the same time.

"There. When you're finished drying off, come out and get your dress on," said Nixson, as he left the bathroom, shutting the door behind him and leaving Samantha standing in the middle of the tub.

Samantha did the best she could, drying herself off. Bruises were deep and dark on her arm where Carl had grabbed her harshly before. She took the dress and began to slip it on herself when she remembered something. The small knife in her pants pocket that she had found back in the van. She rummaged through her pants pocket and found the small pocketknife. Taking it, she found a small pocket on the inside of her dress that was just big enough to hide the knife in. Stuffing the knife into this pocket, she proceeded to put the dress completely on herself.

"How did it go in there?" asked Carl as Nixson walked back out into the office.

"Fine. Once I got her convinced to take a goddamn bath. Had to dump her in at first with all her clothes on. Couldn't get her to take her damn underwear off though."

"Will that be an issue?"

"No, she doesn't need to shave yet. I would imagine she will probably be here in the next year though."

"Well, as long as she doesn't need to shave anything before the auction. Afterwards, I don't care what happens, just as long as she is good to go."

"She will be good to go. When can I expect the next one to come to be cleaned?"

"I don't know."

"What do you mean?"

"I don't know is what I mean."

"Like you're not going to do this work anymore?"

"I don't know. Maybe. Might try to go up to Seattle to find my daughter."

"Finishing the job is what you mean?"

"I don't know. Maybe."

"Still upsets you some, huh?"

"If I had it my way, I would have killed her a long time ago."

"Your ex?"

"Yes."

"And what of your daughter?"

"I don't know. I think about her from time to time."

"Reuniting with her?"

"Punishing her for running away from me."

Nixson chuckled to himself. "You know, you always had a fucked-up mind. For as long as I've known you for, anyway."

"Well, that's what my ex would say to you too, I'm sure."

Both men heard a door open behind them and turned around simultaneously. Samantha walked out of the bathroom in her red dress. Rhinestone jewels adorned the front of the dress, sparkling under the lights. Her brown hair was combed back, and her gaze was cast down to the ground.

"Beautiful. Absolutely stunning," said Nixson as he walked over to her. "If I had the money myself, I would place a bid on her."

He brushed her arm with the back of his hand when he noticed the bruising on her arm.

"Oh dear," he said.

"What is it?" asked Carl.

"Bruising on her arm. Well, we'll just have to get rid of that."

Nixson turned around and walked over to a nearby closet. He opened it and pulled a shoebox down from the top shelf, then a second shoebox. The items within clanked around as he set the box on top of the other box in his arms. Shutting the door with his foot, he turned and walked back over to the bathroom.

"Come, follow me, my child." He walked into the bathroom, and Samantha followed.

Setting the boxes down on the counter, he opened them and sifted through small glass bottles of makeup, looking for the right color to match her skin tone.

"How many bruises do you have on yourself?" asked Nixson.

"Just this one."

"Did Carl do that to you?"

"Yes."

"Well, you won't have to be around him for much longer. Let's hope your future husband doesn't grab you like that either," said Nixson as he held bottle after bottle against the side of her arm to match the skin color.

"There. This one should work," he said as he found the right color of makeup for her skin tone.

Turning around, he set the other small jars down on the counter and grabbed a brush from the box. He opened the jar, set the lid on the counter, then turned and dabbed the brush into the makeup, applying it to her arm and around the bruise.

"There, you see? A perfect match," he said with a smile on his face as he brushed her arm with the makeup, like how Picasso would paint a canvas.

"There you are. You'll be good as new in no time."

"Please help me," she begged quietly.

"I can't do that. There is just too much money involved in this work, and if I helped you, I would lose a payday and then probably even lose my business. So that will not happen. I'm sure you're resourceful; you can figure things out for yourself. You know, I think it would be a good thing that you're going to be bought by a wealthy man. Or woman. You're guaranteed a good life, whereas before, you would be taking a chance with a man outside this community.

Guaranteed money. Wealth. A roof over your head. Really, you should consider yourself very lucky to be in the position that you are right now."

"Trapped? Forced into something I don't want? I haven't gotten the chance to be a teenager yet. I was robbed of my teenage years with my friends. My parents. Proms. Graduations. Campouts. Father daughter dances. Sleepovers. Family holidays and summer vacations. All of it. It all means more to me than money."

"Sure, a child would think that way."

"I am a child."

"You need to grow up and learn that the only thing important in this world is money. Carl knows that. I know that. Harkin knows that. If you would just listen to me and..."

"That's where you're wrong," said Samantha.

Nixson stopped brushing the bruise on her arm and slapped Samantha in the face with the back of his hand.

"Shut the fuck up! And listen to what I have to say. Goddamn it, there's another bruise that I'll have to cover up," he said, dabbing the brush into the makeup jar again.

He violently pushed the brush with the makeup on it into her face, hiding the bright red mark he had left behind from smacking her. Samantha sat there quietly, not saying anything more, afraid of further angering the man.

"There. We're almost done. You know you should refrain from talking back or interrupting your future husband or wife. The best thing for you to do is just accept that this is what the rest of your life will be like."

With the last stroke of the makeup brush, he smiled and set the brush down on the countertop.

"There. Good as new. Listen, I'm sorry that I had to hit you like that. But you really made me do it. You can't talk back. You need to keep your voice quiet."

Samantha sat there quietly, not saying anything, and her eyes downcast towards the bathroom tile floor.

"Come on," said Nixson as he stood up from the edge of the bathtub and walked towards the door.

Samantha stood up behind him, and they walked out of the bathroom together. Carl was sitting in a chair up against the wall when he looked over and saw them both coming up to him.

"What the hell took you so long?" asked Carl.

"Just covering up all the bruises is all. Making her perfect for sale. Perfection is what will bring in high dollars. However, you had best get going soon if you want to make it to the auction in time this evening. Eight o'clock tonight, is it?"

"Appreciate your help, Nixson. I'm sure Mr. Harkin appreciates it as well."

"Don't sell her short of her value, Carl. This one is worth more than you think. A lot more value in one like this."

With that, Carl shook Nixson's hand and informed him that he would let Mr. Harkin know that he did a good job cleaning up and preparing Samantha for the auction this evening. Both Carl and Samantha walked out of the church and back towards their car parked along the side of the street. He opened the passenger door and helped her in.

"Your chariot awaits," he said as he ushered her into the passenger seat.

Samantha slowly got into the car. Carl picked up her dress from the ground and set it on her lap. He reached in and buckled her into the seat, then shut the passenger door, locking it from the outside with his car key.

Walking around the front of the car, he went to the driver's side and got in. Starting the car, he pulled out onto the road, and they began their drive to the Wine and Dine house up in Los Angeles.

Chapter 13: Hollywood Hills, California

The drive from Santa Ana, California, north to Hollywood Hills, California, didn't take much time at all. Carl drove north on Interstate 5 and then onto Highway 101, the great Pacific Coast Highway that ran from southern California all the way up through the Oregon coastline and into Washington state. However, Carl and Samantha weren't going this far. They would be on the road for merely about an hour.

"It won't be much longer now. Once we're there, you're going to go to a room to stay until the auction starts this evening around 8:00 PM. Then once you're sold, I'm taking off, and you'll never have to see me for the rest of your life. I'm sure you'll appreciate that," said Carl while he drove along the interstate, heading north to the Hollywood Hills exit that was still a few miles ahead of them.

"What are you going to do with your portion of the money that you make?" asked Samantha.

"What do you care?"

"Just asking."

"Just fucking live, I guess."

"You going to go up to Seattle when you're done with me?"

"Maybe. Maybe not. Who really cares anyway?"

In that moment, a car darted in front of Carl. Causing him to hit his brakes sharply.

"Goddamn son of a bitch! Jesus, I forget how much I hate traffic in Los Angeles," he said.

"Maybe you shouldn't plan on going to Seattle?" said Samantha.

"Oh yeah? Why is that? You think you're my life coach now?"

"No, I'm just saying. Maybe it might be a situation you emotionally can't handle for yourself yet?"

"Goddamn it, how old are you? You're sitting here, talking to me about life choices? If you want to know so goddamn bad, yes. I'm planning on driving right up Highway 101. Take in some gorgeous views of the Pacific Ocean and the beaches. Cruise right into Astoria, then connect over to Interstate 5. Drive north to Seattle. Find my ex. Kill her. Then find my daughter. Kill her, too. Then probably kill myself. I don't know. Consider yourself lucky I don't kill you for pissing me the fuck off so much these last few days now. The only reason why I don't is because I need the money to travel to kill them up in Washington. So do yourself, and me a favor, and sit there, and shut the fuck up!"

The car went silent for a moment. The only sound was of the tires rolling along the highway. Samantha looked out the passenger window and watched as traffic buzzed by them in the right-hand lane. She looked up and saw million-dollar mansions on top of the hillside, along with houses that were less desirable along the highway, and at the bottom of the hillside.

"Isn't it beautiful?" he asked her, noticing that she was looking out the window now.

"What?"

"The homes. You'll soon learn in life that shit rolls downhill in this world. Got the elite, wealthy at the top of the hill. Then the slums at the bottom. Hardworking men and women, living paycheck to paycheck, struggling to even pay a power bill. Then you got the folks at the top of the hill who have special bottles of champagne flown in from France directly to their homes. While guys like me are barely able to afford off-brand bottles of soda and microwave dinners from the frozen food section. Like I said before, you should consider yourself very lucky that you're in the position you're in here. Maybe you might be living up on that hill soon too."

"It's still not what I want for myself."

"And what do you want for yourself?"

"Freedom."

"Funny. And you're not willing to give up a little of yourself for the best that freedom has to offer?"

"That's not freedom."

"How do you know?"

"I want to be able to make choices. Good ones, and bad ones. To be able to say hey, it worked out or that was a mistake. And I'm sorry."

"And why do you think you want to struggle with the rest of us like that? Why don't you just accept the possibilities for yourself and forgo the hardships?"

"That is where you and I differ. Freedom comes with hardships. The satisfaction of overcoming the hardships is where the biggest feeling of reward comes from."

"Yeah, and who told you that?" asked Carl.

"I've had to do a lot of growing up this past week. All those children back at the farm. Out of the country. Forced into work. Fighting with guns for armies that don't care about their well-being. I guess you could say I see the world in a different light now," said Samantha.

"Well, I'm sorry to be the one to ruin the world and life for you. But at least you now know how cruel the world can be, and how humans can be the worst monsters of them all. Soon enough, my ex and daughter will find that out, too."

"I think they already know," said Samantha, turning and making eye contact with Carl.

A single tear rolled down her cheek. Falling into her lap.

*   *   *   *

Detective Ho walked briskly through the office of the Texas Rangers in their building located in Houston, Texas. Passing computers and printers that were printing off reports. The office was bustling with beeps from devices, office chatter, and rhythmic typing. He walked towards one of the many offices located on the side wall of the large room of cubicles, where he stopped momentarily. Holding his paperwork together, he knocked on the door and waited until he finally heard a voice from the other side that welcomed him in.

Opening the door, Detective Ho greeted his staff sergeant.

"Sergeant James," he said as he looked up and saw Sergeant Richard James sitting behind his hard oak desk and computer in the small office.

"Yes, Detective Ho. You're coming in late this afternoon. I'd figure you would have shut things down and gone home for the weekend by now," said Sergeant James as he looked up from his laptop.

"Normally I would have, but I received an email from the Tucson Police Department."

"Tucson Police Department?"

"Yes, sir. That murder in the bathroom earlier this week outside of Cove, Texas."

"What of it?"

"Do you remember seeing the man and the girl in the video?"

"Yes, I do. He was a balding middle-aged man wearing bifocals and a purple windbreaker."

"That same man was spotted by a soccer mom in a minivan outside a mall in Tucson, Arizona. Dragging a young girl by the arm, violently back to a gold Toyota Camry with a Texas state license plate number that started with the letters B, L, and W."

"BLW? There was a young girl with them at that gas station, was there not?" asked Seargent James.

"Young girl. Short woman. Yes. In fact, now I would say a young girl."

"Did you check the state database for the license plate?"

"We did. Ran the plate numbers a little while ago to see if there were any matches with a Texas state plate that starts with the letters B, L, and W, and a gold Toyota Camry."

"And?"

"Came back registered to John Harkin."

"John Harkin? The chicken egg farmer?"

"The same one. Who lives out there in Sonora on his farm?"

"Harkin, huh? Was the car reported stolen?"

"I checked, and no, it's not."

"I suppose Harkin could have a daughter that age? But from the advertisements in the state for his eggs, he doesn't look anything like a middle-aged man and balding. Or with beard stubble on his face. He takes very good care of himself from what I've seen from his advertisements," said Seargent James.

"Also, not the kind of guy that I would picture driving a Toyota Camry around either."

"Ugh... and I suppose you want to drive out to Sonora this evening and meet with Harkin at his ranch then?"

"I suppose it could wait until next week, but I do think it would be interesting to follow up. Maybe be able to track down a potential murderer. Then I'm still curious about this girl or short woman. How does her role play into the story?"

"Who knows? Maybe it's a short girlfriend?"

"I'm not sure. But it is suspicious enough to dig around some more, I think," said Detective Ho.

"You know what, I would agree. We'll take it up first thing Monday morning and make a trip out to Sonora to see what we can find."

*   *   *   *

The gold Toyota Camry took the Mulholland Drive exit and drove into the Hollywood Hills area. Taking road after road, they ended up on the last road, called Lake Hollywood Drive, where Carl pulled into a large mansion set along the lakefront. Multiple Hollywood elites were standing around the front of the home as limousines pulled up to the porte-cochères of the home and dropped off their wealthy passengers. The men were dressed in fine evening attire, while the women wore expensive dresses accented with crystals and sparkling diamonds. Truly, the most elite of the elite were present.

Carl pulled the gold Toyota Camry around the side of the mansion to a smaller driveway and a door along the side with a man standing by it, holding a digital pad. After parking the car next to the door, Carl got out and shut the door behind him.

"Hey Carl. Harkin got himself another bitch to enter the auction, huh?"

"Sure does. This one is fine, too. Twelve years old. Just entering puberty. Shapes are just starting to show on her body. Still not shaving."

"Virgin?"

"As far as I know, she is."

"Goddamn, he's got himself a good one. That should fetch a very good price."

"Auction still start at 8:00 PM?"

"Sure does."

"How many girls are available?"

"Fourteen. Yours makes number fifteen."

"Good turnout."

"Indeed. A lot of Hollywood elites are here. Actors. Producers. Directors. Even some CEOs from companies in LA."

"No shit? Sounds like it's going to be a fun evening."

"Definitely," said the man as he raised the tablet up to his chest and began to tap on the screen.

"How old did you say she was, twelve?"

"That's right."

The man looked inside the cab of the car through the window, making eye contact with Samantha, who was hesitant to come out.

"Pretty. Brown hair, mid-point of her back?"

"Yes."

"Where is she from?"

"Chicago. Picked her up in Miami on her family vacation?"

The man laughed. "Kidnapping some clients, I see, Carl?"

"Whatever we've gotta do. Harkin had a sexy Mexican bitch he was going to enter as well, but he's going to use her for something else."

"Yeah, I bet he will. Only thing Mexican girls are good for at this age. I suppose white bitches like this, too. Alright, height?"

"About four feet, eleven inches."

"And weight?"

"Eighty pounds, I'd guess."

"Any scars, marks, tattoos, blemishes on the skin?"

"Only the bruise on her arm that Nixson covered up earlier today?"

"Had to manhandle her a bit?"

"She pissed me the fuck off."

"How is Nixson by the way?"

"Good. Still working for Harkin and dressing up his girls. Making good money at that church he's at in Santa Ana."

"Smart bastard, man. With his good looks, he fits right in with being a minister, doesn't he?"

"Yeah, I suppose so. He's been fooling those people for a long time now."

"You know what grade she's in?"

"School? The hell if I know. Grade school, I suppose."

"Both parents in her life?"

"Seemed like it."

"Good. Dad in a daughter's life should raise the price as well. Fuckin don't go crazy that way. She ever have a boyfriend?"

"No, not that I know of."

"Alright. Well, I got most of the information that I needed for the auction then. You want to take her out, bring her through this door. The seventh door on the right down this hallway is hers. Going to have the number seven on it. Put her in there, shut the door, and we'll take care of her from there. You gonna stick around for the auction?"

"Wouldn't miss it for the world. I always like to see everyone so happy when they are bought and how much their lives improve."

"Great. You can have a seat in the back of the room. Mr. Jack likes to make sure everyone who is up front is in proper dress attire."

"Of course. Mr. Jack is still running the auctions here, huh?"

"Has been for almost twenty years now. The elites love the old bastard."

"Yeah, good for him," said Carl as he walked over to the passenger car door and opened it.

"Alright, Samantha. Get out and follow me."

Samantha slowly got out of the car, careful as she walked in heels. It was one of the first times she had worn heels anywhere, and it was quite uncomfortable. She tried not to fall as they walked around the car.

"First time wearing heels, honey?" asked the man.

Samantha ignored him. Holding only herself with her arms as she carefully walked by him, along with Carl. On the way in through the door, the man checked her out from behind.

"Goddamn. He ain't kidding about the curves at twelve," he said as the door closed behind them.

Once inside, Carl and Samantha walked down a long hallway with gold walls. Gold lit oil lamps and oil paintings adorned the walls. Samantha glanced over and read the name on one of the paintings: Pablo Picasso. Red carpet ran down the center of the floor. Samantha stumbled in her high heels as she transitioned onto the carpeted section of the floor.

"You better walk a hell of a lot better than that when you get up on that stage this evening. You're just going to get laughed out of the room and cost Mr. Harkin some money if you're not flawless," said Carl as he looked up and counted the room numbers as they walked by.

"Seven. There it is. Alright, this is your room. This is the last place that I'm ever going to talk to you face to face. After this, you're going to be ushered to the stage on the floor above us by the auction assistant. They'll take you up, have you walk around the stage, and the guests will bid. Then, when the highest bid is received, you'll be brought back here until your buyer comes to pick you up, and then you live happily ever after. The end. You're welcome," said Carl as he opened the door.

Inside the room there was another girl, slightly older than Samantha, who was dressed in a blue dress, sitting quietly on a loveseat sofa.

"Get in," he said as Samantha slowly walked into the room.

Carl shut the door behind her and locked it. The room was painted white with red accents. There was no other door in the room and no window either. Oil lamps provided light along the walls, and a small glass chandelier hung in the center of the room, lighting up the room. She walked up to the girl in the blue dress who was sitting nearby on a leather sofa.

"What's your name?" asked Samantha.

"Elizabeth."

"That's my mom's name. Where do you come from?"

"Gresham."

"Where's that?"

"Oregon."

"How did you end up here?" asked Samantha as she sat down on the couch.

"I ran away from home," said Elizabeth.

"Ran away from home?"

"Yeah. I threatened my parents that I would run away, so I did. I had made it about a block down the road when a woman in a car pulled up next to me and asked me where I was going. I told her I was running away from home, so she invited me to get into her car to go for a ride. So I wanted to get back at my dad for not believing me that I was going to leave, so I got in. She took me to her home down in Eugene, where I worked for her family. Doing things around the house. Cleaning, cooking, laundry. She even gave me to her husband to do things with."

"Do things?"

"I don't want to talk about it. She would watch while he used me."

"I'm sorry to hear that."

"I just want to go home, but when they were finished with me, she brought me down to this house, and I've been in this room for a couple of days now, just waiting for this evening to come. They said because I'm not a virgin anymore that I wouldn't fetch a high price, but I should still make them a profit. I honestly just want to go back home. To my dad. But it doesn't sound like that's ever going to happen again."

"I'm sorry, Elizabeth. Why don't you try to break out and run away?"

"And run where? Where am I going to go? There's a big lake on one side of us, a driveway full of people on one side, a deck with a big grass yard on the other side, and finally a hill on the other side of that."

"You must try."

"It's not worth it. Honestly, it's fine. This is probably the best for me, anyway. It's not like I was going to make a big difference with my life. Maybe this is for the best. It's not so bad being a mistress to a married couple. If it means I get to live comfortably."

"There must be something better to life than just that, Elizabeth. There has to be."

"I don't really care anymore."

"And maybe that's why you don't try?"

Someone knocked on the door, and then a short, stocky man dressed in an evening tuxedo walked in.

"Alright, Elizabeth?" he said.

Elizabeth stood up and walked up to the man.

"Sixteen years old, five-foot one inch. Hundred and ten pounds," he said, looking her up and down. "You're the one. Are you ready?"

The young girl didn't reply as she walked out into the hallway. The man turned around and walked back into the hallway too, when he turned around and stuck his head back into the room.

"I'll be back for you in about ten minutes," he said before he shut the door.

It was the longest ten minutes of Samantha's life as she waited quietly in the room. Through the ceiling, she heard the clamoring of voices and yelling until the room upstairs finally quieted down, going silent. A moment later, the same man from ten minutes earlier entered the room.

"Alright, honey. It's your turn now. Are you ready for your moment?"

Samantha stood up and walked out into the hallway. There, she saw Elizabeth standing next to the man. When Samantha walked out of the room, Elizabeth walked back in. The man shut the door behind her.

"Why is she going back into the room?" asked Samantha.

"She's just waiting to be picked up by her highest bidder at this point. She'll probably be gone by the time you are finished up. There's only one girl per winner here at this show, so the lucky lady will be coming down to pick her up and take her away soon. Come on, follow me and don't fall in those when you're on the stage," he said as he turned around and walked away.

Samantha kept up with him as they approached an elevator at the end of the hallway. The man pushed the button for the elevator, and they walked in as the doors opened. The elevator whisked them up a level to the main stage, where the doors opened and they walked out behind the stage. Samantha heard a lot of loud chatter among the audience, followed by some of the auctioneers who were up at the front. One older man appeared to be in charge of it all, holding a gavel in his right hand. After he finished speaking with one of the auctioneers, he took their tablet and walked back up to a podium on the far side of the stage. Setting the tablet down on the podium, he took the gavel in his hand and hit the sound block on the podium three times.

"Everyone quiet down, we would like to move on to the next girl for the evening. Her name is Samantha, and she comes from Chicago, Illinois," said the lead auctioneer.

"Alright, honey. I'll be right here when they are finished bidding for you. Go ahead and head out there."

Samantha boldly took a couple of steps out onto the stage, bright stage lights focused in on her as she could see the silhouettes of hundreds of men and women in the audience, all dressed fancy and staring at her.

"She is twelve years old, with brown hair that flows down to the center of her back. Properly educated until the age of twelve. Curves in all the right places, even for a twelve-year-old, as you can see. Does not need to shave her body just yet."

When the auctioneer said that, the audience members oohed and aahed.

"There are no blemishes. No serious medical concerns. Her mental health is considered normal as well. Say we start the bidding at $5,000? Do I hear $5,000?"

"$5,000," a voice spoke up from one of the many prospective bidders.

"$10,000," another voice said.

"I have $10,000 now from number thirty-seven. Do I hear $11,000?" said the auctioneer.

"$11,000," said another bidder.

"$15,000."

"$20,000," said yet another bidder.

"$20,000 to number sixteen. Do I hear $21,000?"

"$25,000."

"$30,000."

"$31,000."

"$32,000."

"We have $32,000. $32,000 going once?"

"$35,000."

"Very good! $35,000 is now the bid. Do I hear $36,000?"

In the back of the room, Carl sat in a chair with his back up against the wall, watching as the bidders placed their bids on Samantha. A smile cracked on his face as he realized that Samantha was going to be worth a good amount of money.

"$36,000," said another bidder.

"$37,000."

"$40,000."

"$41,000."

"$41,000 is the bid now. $41,000. Do I hear $42,000?" asked the auctioneer as he scanned the crowd.

"$41,000 going once? Going twice?"

"$42,000."

"$45,000."

Some of the women in the audience gasped as the dollar amount grew. Samantha was drawing in the most money thus far in the night.

"Now, ladies and gentlemen. I draw your attention to this fine specimen of a young woman. Twelve years old. Doesn't even have to shave her body yet, but she's just starting to get her figure. Ripe for the taking. And a virgin! The bid is at $45,000!"

"$50,000."

"$55,000."

"$56,000."

"$60,000."

"$70,000."

"God damn! $70,000 from number twenty-three."

"$80,000."

"$80,000!" yelled the auctioneer. "$80,000 dollars to number forty-six."

"$85,000."

The auctioneer smiled, his lips curled as he said, "$85,000." The audience gasped as they looked around to see if anyone else would bid up on the $85,000 bid when they noticed paddle number eleven raise.

"$95,000."

"$95,000! How about that? $95,000 is the bid now. Do I hear an even $100,000?"

Carl was ecstatic. His payday from Mr. Harkin was looking better and better with each bid.

"Do I hear $100,000?"

Another paddle was raised in the room.

"$100,000."

"$105,000."

"$106,000."

"$107,000."

"$107,000! Do I hear $108,000?"

Side conversations were faintly heard in the room as Samantha stood there on the stage, her life and body being sold like a piece of property.

"$107,000 dollars going once. Going twice." He swung his mallet down onto the sound block, producing a loud crack.

"Sold! To bidder number thirty for $107,000. What a prize. From the looks of it, you won't be disappointed," said the auctioneer with a crooked smile on his face.

With that, the man who had escorted her up to the auction floor came out on the stage, took her politely by the arm as a gentleman would walk a lady, and ushered her off the stage, behind the curtains.

"$107,000. If I saw right, it looked like the actress Sandra Storm was paddle number thirty. That should be exciting for you," he said as he pushed the button to the elevator.

The doors opened, and he ushered Samantha into the elevator. She felt hopeless and trapped as the elevator doors slowly closed in on them, taking them back downstairs to the girls' rooms. When the doors opened, he walked her out into the hallway and back to room number seven. Taking the keys out of his pocket, he unlocked the door and opened it. Looking around the room, he noticed that the other girl was gone already.

"Huh. They must have processed your roommate's bid early and taken her away already. Well, wait here, and shortly your new owner will be here to pick you up too. I would guess maybe ten, fifteen minutes?"

The man turned around and shut the door behind him. The floor creaked under his body weight as Samantha heard him walking away and preparing the next girl by the elevator. Samantha put her ear up to the door and heard the elevator bell as it opened and then closed. She took her ear away from the door and looked closer towards the door jamb and noticed something interesting.

The door wasn't shut all the way against the doorjamb.

Chapter 14: The Wine and Dine

Taking her high heels off, Samantha tossed them into the room behind the sofa. She pulled the door open, revealing the hallway, then quickly shut it as she heard voices approaching from the opposite end of the hallway. She prayed that it wasn't the auctioneers coming for her with the winning bidder. But they stopped two doors down from her at room number five, opened the door for a different winning bidder. When she heard their voices retreat, she opened the door again and stepped out into the hallway. Carefully, she closed the door behind her without making a sound.

Looking up and down the hallway, she saw numbered doors on each side of the narrow hallway, and a door on the west end of the hallway, which led outside to the parking area. She remembered it was the way she'd come in. On the east side of the hallway, there was an elevator that led up to the auction floor. She ran towards the door on the west side that led to the parking lot along the side of the mansion. When she got there, she slightly opened the door and peeked outside, where she saw three men dressed in fine suits, talking with one another, unaware Samantha was only 15 or so feet away.

She slowly shut the door, careful not to make a sound in doing so. She turned around and ran back down the hallway, barefooted, towards the elevator. She was about to push the button and take her chances in the elevator when the elevator dinged. She heard the door opening on the floor above her. Samantha panicked, breathing heavily as she looked for a place to hide from the man who was coming back down to the rooms.

She tried one of the doors at the end of the hallway, and it was locked. However, she tried the adjacent door next to the elevator, and it opened, revealing a small cleaning closet. She quickly darted into the closet and shut the door behind her just as the elevator doors opened. Placing her ear up against the door, she steadied her breathing and stayed quiet as she heard a man walking out of the elevator, along with a girl he was escorting back to one of the rooms.

She carefully opened the door and watched them walk down the hallway. He passed her room and opened the door to room number five when the girl he was escorting started fighting back. Samantha watched as they wrestled a bit in the hallway until the man grabbed her by the hair, then dragged her into the room. Now was her chance.

She quickly darted out of the closet, opened the elevator and darted inside. She pressed the button for the first floor. The elevator lifted her up to the auction floor, and with a ding the doors opened. Samantha found herself backstage in the auction area again. A young girl, even younger than her, wearing a bright yellow dress, was being auctioned off to the audience. Samantha looked around the back room behind the curtain for a way out. She saw a door, but it was a fire alarm exit door, and it would draw way too much attention and lead to her capture.

The elevator doors closed behind her. As a result, the backstage area went dark. She blindly felt her way around backstage equipment, boxes, and clothing racks filled with pants, shirts, and dresses for kids. She slowly removed her dress while she listened to the auction going on, finding pants and a shirt that fit. She got dressed in that and looked for shoes when the elevator doors dinged close by her.

As the elevator door opened, Samantha ducked into the circular clothing rack, getting down on her hands and knees, as she carefully put the shirt over her head to finish changing. She looked out from under the clothes and saw two pairs of legs. One set belonged to the man who was ushering women to the auction stage, while the second set of legs belonged to another victim.

Samantha stayed still, so that she wouldn't draw any attention to herself when she palmed a hard bump in her red dress that she had changed out of. She grabbed the hard object and remembered it was the pocketknife she had been holding onto the entire time. She worked the knife out of the small pocket in the dress she was wearing and stuffed it into her pants pocket.

The auction ended, and the young woman who had been auctioned off walked behind the stage while another girl switched with her. Then, the man escorted the auctioned-off girl back towards the elevator. Pushing the elevator button the doors opened, flooding the backstage area with light. It lit the backstage area long enough for Samantha to see a second door in the backstage that had no exit sign by it.

When the elevator doors shut, Samantha crawled out from under the clothing rack, adjusting her pants and shirt. Unable to find shoes, she turned and ran through the darkness towards the newly discovered door. Feeling around the wall, she found the door bar and pushed it open, stepping out into another hallway. However, this hallway appeared to be in a desolate location in the mansion. Normal-looking doors stood on each side of the hallway compared to what it looked like downstairs, where they kept the girls they were auctioning off. Samantha carefully stepped down the hardwood floor hallway and tried opening the first door she found on the right side of the hallway.

The door opened, and inside the room was what appeared to be a torture chamber. Chains, bullwhips, and tables with handcuffs attached to the ends of them were scattered throughout the room. She saw bamboo sticks and paddles of some kind hanging on a wall. In one corner of the room, there were lights and a video camera that was pointed towards an unmade bed with stains covering the sheets.

Samantha ran over to the first window she saw, pulled the blinds open, and saw she was clearly on the second floor of the building. Opening the window, she poked her head out and looked around. She looked down at the drop-off area at the front of the mansion. People were coming and going from the parking area as a couple of valets would bring cars to waiting guests who were leaving for the night with their purchases. Samantha also watched as a couple of limousines pulled up towards the front, then watched as some prominent actors that she had seen in some movies and even children's movies came out and got into them.

She then heard some loud chatter from down in the front of the mansion and could hear someone saying that "one of the girls was missing from the rooms."

Her heart sank into the pit of her stomach. She pulled back from the window, leaving it open as she listened to someone asking the valets if they had seen a young, twelve-year-old girl with brown hair in a red dress coming outside. She heard the valet tell the man, no. Then she heard an all too familiar voice.

"Do they know where she is?" asked Carl to one of the men downstairs.

"No, they haven't seen her," said one man.

"If we don't find that goddamn kid, we're out $104,000, have a pissed-off actress, and Harkin will probably kill my ass. We find that little bitch, no matter what. You understand me?"

"I got it," said another man.

"Look around the mansion. Upstairs. There's nowhere else she could be."

Samantha's heart pounded hard in her chest. She knew it wouldn't be long before they found her, and when they did, who knew what they would do to her. She had to hide and hide fast. She looked around the room, but there were no closets to hide in. She pulled the blinds back and opened the window and looked around, thinking perhaps she could jump, but from the second level the fall would surely hurt her. Shutting the window, she heard faint footsteps walking down the hallway and opening doors. She quickly took one of the blankets from off the bed in the room, rolled herself up in it and then rolled under the bed, with her back propped up against the wall. The smell from the bed sheets nearly made her gag, but there were no other options. As soon as Samantha was in position, she heard the door to her room open. Light from the hallway poured into the room, along with a man's shadow.

Carefully, she peeked one eye out through the blanket, watching from under the bed as the man walked into the center of the room. He walked towards the corner, then stopped and looked around, listening for her. She saw he was one of the men that Carl was talking to from outside in the porte-cochères. He walked up to one of the paddles that hung on a hook on the wall. Taking the paddle down, he inspected it, then brought the paddle up to his face and licked it, giving a satisfied grunt of approval as he finished. He hung the paddle back up on the wall, turned around and walked out of the room. Shutting the door behind him. Outside in the hallway, she heard voices.

"You found her yet?" Carl asked.

"No, nothing yet," replied the man who had just been in the room with her.

"Goddamn it. Well, keep looking. She has to be here somewhere."

The sound of footsteps walking down the hallway, away from her room, spurred Samantha into motion. She uncovered herself and crawled out from under the bed, and walked over towards the door. She cracked the door open and peered into the empty hallway. With the coast clear, she exited the room and softly closed the door behind her. The hallway was quiet. She wasn't even able to hear the sound of the audience in the auction room anymore. Quickly, she tried the door on the opposite side of the room she had been in, but it was locked. She grunted as she tried to turn the knob, but it was of no use. The door wouldn't budge.

She backed away from the door and walked down the hallway past a pallid bust of the goddess Athena, which was sitting nicely on a beautiful marble display stand. Next to the decorative piece was another door. Reaching out, she turned the doorknob, and the door clicked open, revealing a large office area with the lights turned off. She walked in quietly, then shut the door behind her.

On one side of the room was a large oak desk with a computer setup, and filing cabinets standing behind it. A custom-built bookshelf spanned the whole length of the wall across from the desk. The behemoth bookshelf was filled from top to bottom with old hardbound books. Samantha walked over to the bookshelf and removed one of the books and read the title out loud to herself.

"The Cabin at the End of Herrick Road?" she said quietly, looking at the cover and then the back of the book.

She put the book back on the shelf where she had found it when she heard a door open from somewhere out in the hallway. She gasped, turned to look at the door and saw a shadow underneath it. She ran towards the desk on the opposite side of the room and ducked underneath it.

The door opened, and someone flicked the light on as they walked in and looked around. Samantha flattened her body against the floor, looking under the crack in the desk, spotting a pair of men's legs standing in the room. She recognized the old, faded blue jeans. It was Carl.

He scanned the room as he explored the room, checking behind the blinds and furniture. Then, he turned his attention to the desk. Samantha's heart pounded in her chest as she held her breath, knowing she was going to get caught. But as Carl was about to check behind the desk, a man came running into the room from the hallway.

"Carl!"

Carl stopped before he saw Samantha behind the desk.

"What is it?" he asked.

"I think we found where she went, but we need to hurry. I think she got outside," said the man.

"Fuck! $104,000 or not, I'm going to kill that goddamn kid when I find her!" yelled Carl as he turned and ran back towards the door.

The two men ran out of the room together, leaving the door open behind them. They sprinted down the hallway, and out a door that must have led them downstairs.

Samantha took a deep breath, kept her eye on the door and was starting to walk out when another man walked into the room. This man looked like a professional in business attire, followed by another man who was dressed in evening formal attire and carrying a briefcase with him. A woman in a blue dress followed them into the room, too. None of them seemed like they were looking for her and were simply trying to find a room for privacy.

"Shut the door," said the first man to the woman, who promptly complied.

"Alright. So what are you thinking?" asked the business-dressed man who first entered the room.

The second man walked over to the desk, setting down his briefcase with a loud thump. Opening the case, he began to get paperwork out.

"The Swiss account overseas in Europe is all set up for you. Under the fake name of Travis James McMilliman. In four days, Merril Roche and Regeneration pharmaceutical stocks are going to drop to their lowest point in the fiscal quarter. Merril Roche will drop to $1.19 a share. Meanwhile, Regeneration will drop all the way to $.87. The moment it hits $1.19 and $.87 a share respectively, buy and buy as much as you can," said the second man, as he set papers down on the desk.

The other man walked up to the desk as Samantha watched their fancy feet shuffle from underneath. She saw a faint outline of the legs of the woman in the dress on the other side of the wall looking at the books, paying no attention to what the two men were discussing. The second man, who was talking about stocks and buying things, began to speak again.

"Merril Roche is about to secure a contract with one of the largest hospital networks in the country that operate hospitals from the east to the west coast, James Hogan Regional Network. They're going to be the sole providers of pharmaceuticals in the hospitals for patients, nursing staff, and doctors. Their stock is predicted to shoot up to nearly two hundred dollars a share. Maybe more. Nevertheless, though, significantly more than just $1.19 a share."

"In four days, you say?"

"Four days. Wednesday morning they will be announcing their partnership with the James Hogan Network, and when they do, come Friday afternoon you're going to be sitting on a stock worth more than two hundred a share."

"And what about Regeneration?"

"Regeneration is prepared to have a pharmaceutical drug approved to cure paralysis called RJ90," said the man with the briefcase.

"What the fuck is that?"

"RJ90 is a new pharmaceutical drug that has been proven in their testing to cure paralysis. The fucking vegetables from auto accidents, broken necks from diving into the pool headfirst, falling off a ladder and paralyzing yourself. It's proven to work in curing it."

"You're shitting me."

"I shit not. The company is introducing the drug at their second quarter shareholders' meeting in Minneapolis, Minnesota, on Tuesday of next week, and the moment they make the announcement it means one thing."

"What's that?"

"They hold all the power with the drug. Set their prices. And people will pay for it, if they ever have a desire to use their legs, dicks and whatever else is paralyzed. Regardless of how much it is."

"Won't insurance approve it just yet?"

"Insurance companies have already approved it. This company is going to rake every health insurance company and every patient over the coals to give them the chance to walk again."

"Amazing."

"Isn't it? And what it means for you, my Polack friend, is that their stock, which will hit a low of $.87 next Monday, is going to skyrocket the moment RJ90 is made available to the public across the country. Which will be shortly after the shareholder meeting in Minneapolis."

"How high do you think the stock will rise?"

"Almost four hundred dollars a share."

"Jesus Christ!"

"You buy even just five hundred dollars of that stock at $.87 on Monday morning; you're going to profit nearly $230,000 by Friday."

"God bless you, Stanley. I'll contribute a few thousand dollars to that one."

"If you've got the money, now is the time to invest in Merril Roche and Regeneration. Everything you got," said the man, picking up papers and handing them to the second man. "By Friday of next week, you and your wife there could be multimillionaires. Simply on two stocks. Just like that."

"We could easily get that vista in Portofino, Italy, that we had always talked about," said the woman. "Overlooking the harbor and all the luxurious yachts."

"We certainly could. Sounds like a deal to me, Stanley. We buy Monday, is it?"

"We buy Monday. Just swing by my office with your cash, and we'll go over the details and my share for doing the buying and selling."

"Sounds good to me. Your office still over there on Sunset Blvd.?"

"Sure is. Over in the complex by the Film School, 6353 Sunset."

The second man shook hands with the first man and agreed to meet first thing Monday morning. The man with the briefcase took all the paperwork back and stuffed it into his suitcase.

"So, what are you and your wife up to this evening?" asked the man with the briefcase.

"I don't know. Catch what's left of the auction. Maybe find and bid on a play toy for us. Then dump her off onto the street when we're done with her."

"Just a one-time use thing?"

"Now, that I didn't say."

Both the men laughed and walked towards the door. Finally, the three of them left the room, turning off the lights and shutting the door behind them. Samantha wasn't sure what they were talking about and didn't fully understand the concept of stocks or buying and selling. Regardless, now was her time to make a move as she got out from under the desk, ran towards the door and opened it slightly.

She looked out into the hallway and noticed that it was clear. She stepped out into the hallway, shut the door behind herself, and ran down the hallway, passing the other rooms as she went.

She opened the door at the end of the hallway, which led to a staircase. She began her descent to the first floor when she heard the door just below her open, along with Carl's voice.

He stopped when he opened the door and continued talking to whomever it was he was talking to. Samantha figured it was one of the other men who were looking for her, too. She stopped in place and listened as she heard footsteps on the steps beneath. Quickly, she turned and ran back through the second-floor door, into the hallway. Carl heard the commotion on the flight of stairs just above him and began to run up the stairs.

"Stay here! Make sure no one leaves through this door," he said as he ran up the stairs to the second floor.

He burst through the second-floor door and back into the hallway, only stopping for a moment when he noticed the door to his right was opened slightly. Carl smiled, then slowly pushed the door open. The room was large, filled with darkness and furniture: a bed, couch, recliner, television set, and a dresser set with a tall mirror on a swivel stand. Carl stepped into the center of the room, neglecting to turn the light on.

"I tell you what, Samantha. I hope you enjoyed your tour of the second level of this mansion. I really do. It's a beautiful place, isn't it? You could have had this. All of it. Except now you decided to play around and cost Mr. Harkin $104,000 dollars because you weren't ready to go when your owner came to pick you up," he said as he slowly moved about the room, checking behind the couch first, then the recliner.

"For some reason, you really aren't interested in the rich and famous lifestyle. When all you had to do was just lay back and let it happen. You'd rather try to go back home. To Chicago. To be with your parents, who probably will never amount to anything in their lives. And you had it all. You could have been something so much more," said Carl as he walked towards the closet door in the bedroom.

Reaching out, he grabbed the handle to the door, pulled it open and looked inside the walk-in closet. She wasn't there.

"But I like you, Samantha. You remind me of my daughter. And when this is all over, I'm going to take care of her like I'm going to take care of you. So I'll make a deal with you. If you come out now, and come to me, I promise that I will kill you quickly and painlessly. You have my word on that," he said as he slowly walked out of the closet.

The last place to look was under the bed now. Slowly, he made his way over to the side of the bed.

"But if you don't come out, and I have to find you and catch you, I can promise you that you will die slowly. Painfully. You will hurt, and it will be the last thing you feel in this life," he said as he kneeled down and looked under the bed.

She wasn't there. However, he saw her from across the hallway in the room opposite the one he was in now. The door had swung wide open on its own, revealing Samantha as she was crawling out of an open window, toward a downspout to the rain gutter that ran along the side of the window. She was going to climb the rain gutter down to the ground.

"You goddamn bitch!" he yelled as he stood up and ran around the bed, out of the room and towards Samantha, who was outside, climbing down the gutter.

He reached out through the open window, trying to grab her in the process, but she was just out of his reach, making her way down towards the ground.

"I'm going to kill you!" he yelled as he disappeared back into the room.

Samantha assumed that he was now running back downstairs to the backyard now to try to catch her. She climbed as quickly as she could before she jumped the rest of the way. She landed with a hard thud on the ground, stunning herself for a moment. When she came to, she regained her footing on bare feet and sprinted through the grass, towards the trees around the lake.

She glanced over her shoulder and saw Carl running out of the mansion and into the yard after her.

She ran into the trees to hide. Stepping on stones, twigs, and thistles as she went. The pain in the bottoms of her feet was unbearable, but the thought of being caught by Carl and what could happen to her if she were caught kept her going. She finally found a spot where a bush allowed for a perfect hiding place for her to hide under, just off the small dirt trail that she was on. She lay down in the dirt and crawled under a bush and stayed as quiet as she possibly could. It was only a matter of moments when she heard footsteps approach her position in the darkness. They stopped along the trail for a moment and stood near her. Samantha started to feel the ground around when she found a baseball-sized rock nearby that she took into her left hand.

"You know something? I'm going to be honest with you, Samantha. Since you seem to know me so goddamn well, and you've never met me before in your life. I've been lying to you about something for quite a while now," said Carl, as he walked around the area near her. She could faintly make out a dark silhouette amongst the trees and bushes around them, keeping an eye on that shadow as it moved about the area. Checking bushes and behind trees.

"You see, the truth is that my ex never left me. Neither did my daughter. They aren't in Seattle. And I'm not going to Seattle when I'm finished here. The truth is, I'm going to go find the next girl for Harkin. I'm gonna bring the little bitch here to this auction, and next time we're gonna make some good money. You want to know what happened to my ex and our daughter, though?" said Carl as he continued to check around the trees and bushes.

"Like I said, they never left me. Willingly. In fact, I'm a bit surprised that my ex hasn't been found yet. I met Mr. Harkin around the time my daughter was your age. The opportunity to make good money was there, and money was something I didn't have much of at the time. Still don't but certainly doing better than I was back then. So I sold my daughter. You heard that right. I put her up for auction here at this very mansion you were put up for auction at, and she brought Mr. Harkin in a substantial amount of money. It was so much fun that I started to make a living out of it. Kidnapping children like you wherever I could, bringing them here and to dozens of other auction houses around the country, and selling them for a substantial profit. You think this is the only auction house there is? There are auction houses everywhere. In every state, province, and country. So then she went to be with her new family for life."

Carl continued to walk around the area as he got closer to the bush that Samantha was hiding under.

"And as for my ex. Well, she was less receptive to the idea of my daughter being put up for auction. So I did the only thing I could have done with her. I took care of her. Dumped her body out in the middle of the Great Basin Desert in Nevada. To this day, no one has found her. Not even her own family. Which is fine. They never really liked me, anyway. So fuck'em, right?"

Carl was very close to Samantha now. She watched as his shadow drew closer and closer to where she was hiding. With a last desperate attempt to avoid being caught, she threw the rock from under the bush. It landed down the side of a small hill, crashing through the brush. Carl stopped in place and listened intently.

"Just so you know, my deal still stands," he said as he walked past the bush where Samantha was hiding and towards the sound caused by the rock away from her.

"You will still die when I find you, though. I can promise you that," he said as he pushed his way through the bushes, away from Samantha's position.

When he was out of the area, Samantha took advantage of the moment and crawled out from underneath the brush and headed up the trail, careful not to make a sound as she went. The bottoms of her feet were killing her. The pain was unbearable as she took each step. The rocks, twigs, and thistles on the ground punctured the soles of her feet as she went. After wandering down the trail for a while, she heard cars nearby—a road with traffic on it.

A sense of hope that she was going to make it out of this nightmare fueled her escape. As she started to run, a hand grabbed the back of her hair from behind and yanked her down to the ground. She landed hard on her back, hitting the back of her head on the ground. She felt dizzy. Pain radiated through the back of her head, her scalp warm and wet now.

Samantha looked up and saw Carl standing above her. He stomped her in the stomach with his foot, causing immediate pain in her torso that nearly made her vomit.

"I told you I would catch you, stupid little bitch," he said as he mounted her and wrapped both his hands around her throat.

"And I also told you that I was going to kill you for costing me $104,000 goddamn dollars!" he yelled as he squeezed.

Samantha felt it was impossible to get any air into her lungs at this point, and the radiating sensation in the back of her head began to go numb as she felt her body starting to go limp as she attempted to pry Carl's hands away from her neck. However, he was too strong, and she was unable to break his grip. Her consciousness faded as stars blurred her vision. A mix of panic and helplessness was accompanied by a profound sense of vulnerability as she lay on the cold ground, life fleeting.

In the last moment before she passed out, she remembered the pocketknife that she had in her pants pocket. She reached down into her pocket, opened the knife and swung for Carl's face in one last-ditch effort to survive.

The knife made swift contact with Carl's neck, slicing into the side of his neck and down into his throat. He gasped, not expecting Samantha to have a knife. He released his grip as oxygen rushed back into Samantha's lungs. She coughed and gagged as she tried to catch her breath. Her hair was covered in dirt, leaves, and twigs as she rolled over to her side.

Carl leaned back, but still was on top of Samantha. He grabbed his throat as blood poured from the gash in his neck. He tried to talk, but the wound rendered such a feat impossible. Blood squirted from the sides of his hand, onto Samantha's shirt and pants as he fell backwards onto the ground in a sitting position.

Blood drained from Carl's neck. A profound sense of weakness and disorientation set in, accompanied by a chilling realization of the impending danger. Ironically, it was the same feeling that Samantha had experienced when he was choking the life out of her. His heart raced to compensate for the loss of blood, yet his body began to succumb to shock, leading to a gradual fading of consciousness.

In his final moments, a haunting stillness enveloped his mind as he stared back at Samantha, watching as she leaned up from the ground to look at him. His struggle for life diminished, leaving behind a stark awareness of his impending mortality. Carl's eyes rolled into the back of his head as he lay down on the ground and died. A pool of blood formed around his head and shoulders, trickling from the gash in his neck.

Samantha rolled over and picked herself up off the ground and walked past him. Dropping the knife on the ground next to him, she continued up the trail for a little way until she saw a road. Stumbling out onto the sidewalk, she lay down. The front of her shirt and pants were covered in blood, and her hair was a matted mess. Cars passed her one by one on the road until one driver saw her lying on the sidewalk in blood-soaked clothes and stopped. He ran around the front of his car with his cell phone in hand and called 911 as Samantha lay on the sidewalk, crying.

Chapter 15: Return to Chicago, Illinois

The ride home was gentle, muffled by the soft hum of the engine on the roadway. Samantha, who was exhausted from the entire ordeal, rested her head against the window of Chicago police Detective Ed McAllister's police vehicle. Detective McAllister watched Samantha through the rearview mirror as she rested comfortably in the back seat of the car, both guardian and guide as he drove her back to her home in Park Forest—a small suburban village south of Chicago, Illinois.

They spoke quietly with one another as he drove. Detective McAllister shared stories about his own childhood, about courage, and the power of coming home. Samantha's responses to the detective were soft but grew stronger with each mile, her spirit rebuilding itself after being stretched so thin for the past week. She asked about her parents, Anthony and Elizabeth, and if they were angry. Detective McAllister reassured her that love only grows stronger in absence, that her family had never once stopped giving up on her being alive or seeing her again someday.

Samantha looked out the window of the car and saw the road sign welcoming people to Park Forest, Illinois. Where you could live, grow, and discover. Samantha did a lot of that in the past week. Finding ways to live, grow from the experience, and discover that the world around her was not the perfect place that school made it out to be. While driving, they passed buildings and parks that she recognized, including houses and stores that she and her mom had frequented together.

At the Owen residence, the air was thick with anticipation. For a time, Elizabeth and Anthony never thought they would see their daughter Samantha again. When the call came in from the Chicago Police Department that Samantha was found in Hollywood Hills, California, mixed feelings of shock and relief overcame them. How she was merely steps behind them at the theme park in Miami and then found on the west coast in California overwhelmed them with emotion.

Every car that passed outside in front of their house sent them both rushing to the front door and window. Every phone call made hearts leap and then fall when a telemarketer would ask them about their interest in donating to a political cause. The residence for a solid week had become a sanctuary of sleeplessness: coffee cups stacked beside coloring books, a tangle of blankets on the couch, neighbors and friends huddled together in solidarity with them as they slowly lost hope that they would ever see their daughter again. Until the phone call came in.

Anthony and Elizabeth clung to each other, voices hushed as they replayed her laughter in their minds, terrified of forgetting even a moment while they waited as patiently as possible. Hoping that she would be found by someone. They had given interviews, pleaded on local TV, and left the porch light on every night. A beacon of hope in the darkness of the night for their missing child.

When the police detective's vehicle finally turned onto their road, a hush settled over the house. Detective McAllister parked in their driveway as Samantha peered out at the familiar world she had known before she left on her vacation.

The detective parked the car and opened her door, crouching down to her level and offering a hand. She took it, her grip surprisingly strong. Together, they walked up the driveway. Each step was heavy with the gravity of what was about to unfold for Samantha.

The front door opened before they reached it. Anthony and Elizabeth surged forward, laughter and tears mingling as they enveloped their daughter. Samantha clung to them both, her small arms fierce and desperate, as if she could anchor herself to safety by sheer force of will. The detective stepped back, letting the reunion bloom in its own time, a witness to a sacred love that only parents and children would know.

Neighbors cheered softly from across the street, a chorus of joy that carried on the afternoon air, as they crossed the street and walked over to the Owen residence to welcome Samantha home. The neighborhood of Park Forest seemed to exhale, the tension dissolving as Samantha was cradled by those who had missed her the most.

Detective McAllister lingered at the edge of the yard, watching the family's joy expand and overcome every shadow that fear had left behind. It wasn't often that police work permitted moments like this. A conclusion to a horror story, etched in light instead of dark. Even though he didn't have much to do with the investigation, the detective felt the ache of exhaustion and the quiet pride of a mission fulfilled—the belief that every child deserves to come home. Before slipping away into the car and leaving the family be, Detective McAllister paused, glancing back at the reunited family. The job was rarely easy; the outcomes too often uncertain. But tonight, hope had won.

Anthony stood up from his crouched position and ran over to the detective as he was opening the door to his police vehicle.

"Wait, hold on!" he yelled.

"Yes, sir?" the detective replied.

"I just wanted to say. Thank you for bringing my daughter safely back home to us."

"Don't thank me. I can give you the phone numbers of the detectives and officers who found her, and you can thank them. I just met her at the airport and brought her home is all."

"How was she found?"

"I don't know whether I can share that with you or not."

"Detective. Please."

The detective sighed as he opened his door, resting his left arm on the door and right arm on the roof of the car.

"She was found in the Hollywood Hills, California, on a street sidewalk covered in blood. Not her blood. We presume the blood of the kidnapper."

"What happened?"

"She was going to be sold into human trafficking. Sex work. Local detectives and now the FBI found a home there in the neighborhood that was holding auctions for kidnapped girls. And I mean young girls. Pre-teens, early teens. Selling them into forced marriage, sex labor, you name it. She had escaped somehow and managed to get away. Allegedly, her captor tried to strangle her to death. But she took a pocketknife out and tried to stab him with it, but ended up cutting the guy's throat and killing him. Then she made her way up to a public road, found help, and that's how we got her," said the detective.

"I can't believe this happened," said Anthony as Elizabeth and Samantha went back into the house together.

"That's just half the story. There's more to it. However, I already told you too much. The investigation is still ongoing, and we feel after what your daughter shared with us this is a part of a bigger operation of kidnapping girls and selling them into sex trafficking. So, with all due respect, Mr. Owen, I'm going to retire for the afternoon and call it a day."

"If you learn more, will you tell me?"

"The most I can do is give you the lead agent's name with the FBI. Whatever more he shares with you that I haven't yet is at his discretion."

The detective leaned into the car, grabbed his work phone and looked up the name and contact phone number for the FBI agent in charge of the investigation. Detective McAllister, however, reminded Anthony that they probably would not share a lot of information with him yet, as the investigation was still ongoing. Anthony took down the information on his phone, thanked the detective for bringing his daughter back home and shook his hand. Both men smiled at each other as they shook hands.

Samantha struggled to heal, though. Over time, she slowly folded her ordeal into the tapestry of her life. Each moment of the horror etched into her memory replayed every night when she shut her eyes and went to bed. Nightmares woke her up in the early morning hours. Her laughter never returned to its former brightness. Anthony and Elizabeth would find themselves checking on her a little more often, holding her hand a little more tightly, cherishing every ordinary moment that they now had together. But things were never like they used to be for Samantha.

Epilogue: Forever Nightmares

13 years later…

A young 25-year-old woman hesitated at the entrance of the Thompson's Therapy Clinic in Racine, Wisconsin. Her heart was racing with a mix of embarrassment and trepidation. Her childhood was perfect until the summer she was twelve. Each step after that point was heavy as she forced herself to confront the haunting memories of her past, day after day. Haunted memories hounded her in her private moments. The moments when there was nothing but quiet. They disrupted her sleep every night as she woke up to nightmare after nightmare. As if they were on repeat every single night she slept. It had been years since she had gotten a full night's rest. Her painful history was marked by exploitation and trauma.

The thought of discussing her experiences of being trafficked for sex and slavery filled her with dread, even having established a decent working relationship with her therapist of the past eleven years. It never got any easier confronting her past. Yet she understood that facing these demons was essential for her healing. With a deep breath, she toughened herself for the journey ahead, determined to reclaim her narrative and find a path toward recovery.

Opening the door, Samantha stepped into the clinic as she was greeted by the receptionist who had known her from previous encounters.

"Hi, Sam. How are you doing today?" She asked with a smile on her face.

"Fine. Just coming in for my 5:30 appointment with Dr. Lee," replied Samantha.

"Sounds good," said the receptionist as she turned to the computer. "Are you still with Regent Health?"

"Yes, I am."

"How is work going?"

"It's fine. Just getting used to how things work with the state of Wisconsin."

"I bet it's rewarding working with children the way that you do."

"Sure."

"Well, I have you checked in. Now that you're here, I'm going to go ahead and head home for the night. Dr. Lee will make sure you get out okay when you're finished with your session this evening."

"Sounds good. Thank you for being flexible with me and seeing me after hours unexpectedly like this. I just needed to talk to someone. The feelings came back really bad today. I saw a van in the shopping market lot that reminded me of the van."

"It's no problem at all, Sam," said the receptionist as she logged out of her computer for the evening.

She grabbed her purse and stood up, then walked around the corner of the front counter.

"It's amazing how our brains work. The slightest smells, sights, tastes, touches. They trigger memories that, no matter how hard you try to suppress them and heal from them, just continue to rear their ugly heads. I hope you have a good session, Sam. You can go ahead and go back to Dr. Lee's office. You know where it is. When you're finished, have a good night."

"Thanks. You too," said Sam, forcing a smile on her face.

The receptionist smiled back, then turned and walked towards the front door of the clinic. She pushed it open, walked out, and then removed her keys from her purse and stuck the key in the door, locking it behind her.

Samantha turned and walked down a long hallway to the back, where Dr. Lee's office was. The moment she took a step into the hallway, memories flooded her mind of the time she was in the mansion in the Hollywood Hills, playing a game of cat and mouse with her kidnapper. She paused for a moment there in the hallway. Her breathing intensified as she hyperventilated. Clutching her chest, she leaned her back up against the wall, trying to catch her breath and control her racing heart when she heard a voice from the end of the hallway speak up to her.

"Sam, are you alright?" asked Dr. Lee, stepping out of her office and out into the hallway.

"I just need a minute."

Dr. Lee walked down the hallway towards her, placing her hand on Samantha's shoulder.

"Everything is going to be okay, Sam. Take deep breaths in…and out. No one is here but you and I, and you know I will take care of you."

"I know," she said as she finally began to control her breathing.

"Would you like to walk with me to my office?"

"Alright," she said as Dr. Lee took her by the hand and walked with her together back to her office.

Once in her office, Samantha sat down on a leather loveseat against the wall, while Dr. Lee sat in her office chair behind her desk. She had Samantha's file of their work they had done together over the past eleven years out on her desk, pulling the notes from the most recent session.

Dr. Lee's office was dimly lit, yet her voice was steady and compassionate as she addressed Samantha, a survivor of unimaginable trauma that no human should go through. Especially a child. Samantha's eyes reflected a deep well of pain as she re-lived her harrowing experiences in her memories. For the past eleven years, each word from Samantha had been laced with sorrow and disbelief. Dr. Lee always listened intently, acknowledging the complexity of her life story while gently guiding her towards the possibility of healing. The air was thick with unspoken fears and the struggle for hope, revealing the profound impact of trauma on Samantha's own spirit and the critical need for understanding and support in the journey toward recovery from her childhood trauma.

"So, the last time you and I spoke was a week ago." Dr. Lee started the conversation with.

"It was," replied Samantha as she stared down towards the floor, hesitant to make eye contact with Dr. Lee.

"We weren't scheduled to meet until October 15th. We're two weeks away from that. Was there something that happened that triggered your fears?"

"Yes."

"What was it?"

"I was sitting at the stoplight of Bluemound and 44th. That red light there."

"I'm familiar with the intersection. Over by the Piggly Wiggly store, yes?"

"Yes, that's right. But I was just sitting there, and a white van crossed the intersection."

"And that triggered memories of when you were first kidnapped and stuffed into the kidnappers' van, yes?"

"It did."

"Our brains are remarkably complex. How they can exhibit unpredictable behavior and responses. This intricacy often leads to surprising emotional and cognitive patterns, illustrating the brain's capacity for both creativity and chaos. Understanding these dynamics is essential for navigating mental health challenges and fostering personal growth."

"And that's what I want. I just want to heal."

"I understand. Was there something else that triggered your emotional response to stimuli?"

"The movie I watched a couple of nights ago had a lot of blood in it. There was even a scene where the man slapped the woman, too."

"Perhaps you should try to avoid television shows or movies like that?"

"I thought I would be okay."

"It sounds like the movie may have prepped you for the trauma you experienced from the white van in the intersection."

"When will it end, Dr. Lee?"

"Sam?"

"When will it end? We've been in therapy together for eleven years now. Since I was graduating middle school and starting my freshman year of high school. I thought I would grow out of it and forget about it during my high school years. I didn't. I thought maybe in my college years, being exposed to a new life on my own would help. It didn't. I thought maybe moving north here to Racine and away from Illinois for a bit would be helpful. It wasn't. My parents have always been supportive. Since day one before I was kidnapped, and even more after. But this week, in the summer that I was twelve years old. This goddamn week. Why did it have to be me?"

"That's not fair to ask yourself that question, Sam. You had no control over what had happened. You certainly never intended to put yourself in a position where you would experience what you had."

"I have nightmares?"

"You still do?"

"Every night."

"Tell me more about them."

"I'll tell you about the last one. I was hiding under a bed in a dark room. I don't know how long I had been there, but it was like I had woken up from my sleep and there I was. The floor was cold and dirty. There were leaves, twigs, rocks, and grass under the bed. I laid there on my back, quietly and simply waited."

"Waited? For what, Sam?"

"I didn't know at first, but while I was under the bed, the door to the bedroom opened, and I watched from under the bed as black shoes and jeans approached the bed. They stopped by the bed, merely inches from my face, and then I could feel whoever it was get up on the bed. The body weight of the person pressed me down into the floor, and I couldn't move. I was stuck. Then I felt hands come through the mattress and grab me by the neck and choke me, and the bed mattress forced me down to the ground. I couldn't breathe, and just as I was passing out from being choked out, I woke up. I sat up in bed and took a big breath. With the light on the bedstand next to me, I turned it on and looked around my bedroom, but it was just me there. There was no one else. I wasn't under the bed, but it felt so real, and it truly felt like I wasn't able to breathe."

"Certainly, sounds like a nightmare to me. And what did it remind you of?"

"Everything. I sometimes feel that society casts its eyes on me and disapproves. Sometimes I feel ashamed and isolated because of it."

"How is your relationship with Aaron going?"

"We broke up over the weekend. Every time I'm touched, it just reminds me too much of the past. I know he would never do anything to hurt me. Or take advantage of me. I just can't let that barrier down."

"You two were doing so well for the past three months now."

"We were."

"Would you like to talk more about that?"

"I just don't think I'm ready for an intimate relationship yet. Especially one that is so trusting."

"Just because of intimacy?"

"I can't satisfy him the way a woman should be able to. I can't satisfy anyone. On top of that, I still feel I can't trust anyone either."

"You must first learn how to satisfy yourself. Take care of your life first."

"That's what he said as well. Said he wasn't going to give up that easily on me."

"And what do you think of that?"

"Scared."

"Tell me more about that."

"Why doesn't he want to just give up on me? All boyfriends I've had in the past would have walked away by now. I would have been too much of a hassle. A headache to them."

"Perhaps he's different? Care more about you than you realize."

"I'm just thinking if I'm still not past my issues, then will I ever be?"

"That's entirely up to you," said Dr. Lee, as she stood up and walked around the corner of her desk, leaning up against the front of it.

"Some survivors of human trafficking never recover. They never fully heal. They merely cope with the pain. The memories. Yes, human trafficking survivors can and do recover emotionally, but it is a complex and often lengthy process," said Dr. Lee.

"Eleven years now and I'm still fucked in the head," said Samantha.

"I wouldn't put it that way, Sam. The trauma endured during trafficking can have profound and lasting psychological effects, but with support and resources, survivors can find healing and rebuild their lives. Even you. Perhaps Aaron is different. Maybe he's exactly what you need to rebuild. It's perfectly fine to embrace help and support along the way. Especially from someone who wants to be there like that. You know we've talked about this before, but trafficking can severely damage a survivor's sense of self-worth, making it difficult to envision a life free from exploitation."

"And that's what scares me. What if he just exploits me? Am I strong enough to see that, but say no at the same time?"

"And what if he won't? What if he's the person who was sent in life to be your support and your anchor?"

Samantha sat back on the couch, resting the back of her head on the backrest.

"You want me to give him a second chance, I take it?"

"I don't want you to do anything you don't want to do. All I am saying is that maybe you should give him a chance to prove his worth in your life."

"It's so hard," said Samantha, emotionally distraught.

"I know it is. But I will be here for as long as it takes for you."

Samantha sat on the couch; a couple of tears fell from her eyes into her lap.

Dr. Lee walked over to Samantha and sat next to her now.

"You know, one of my favorite psychologists in history, Dr. Abraham Maslow, once said that in any given moment, we have two options in our lives: to step forward into growth, or to step back into safety. I've had a lot of time in my life to ponder this quote as a clinician, and I often found in his work on self-actualization and human motivation to be exact, he perfectly illustrates the ongoing process of personal growth and the choices we make between comfort and risk in life."

"I haven't felt comfort in my life in a long time," said Samantha.

"Maybe in order to find comfort, you'll have to make yourself uncomfortable."

"I can't believe I'm going to say it, but okay. I'll call him back and talk with him and try harder."

"We can talk more about it if you'd like to, Sam?"

"No, I'm going to try."

"What else is on your mind? How are your parents?"

"Doing well. Still living in Chicago."

"Park Forest, is it?"

"Yeah. They stay in touch with me, and my dad calls and checks in on me all the time, too."

"You're doing better than most survivors of trafficking, you know that?"

"Doesn't feel like I am."

"You are. You have loving parents who are genuinely concerned about your well-being. You're willing to come to therapy routinely. Then you have a boyfriend that wants to be there to help you grow from the sounds of it. You're doing better than most survivors."

"Yeah, I suppose I might be doing a bit better than most."

"I have something for you," said Dr. Lee, smiling as she stood up.

Walking back over to her desk, she picked up a piece of paper and then turned around. Walking back to Samantha, she handed her the paper to look at.

"There is a new group meeting I am holding for survivors of human trafficking next month. I have a total of six survivors and was hoping that you would be the seventh."

Samantha took the paper, read it over, and smiled.

"Every second and fourth Thursday of the month at 5:00 PM, starting on the 17th?"

"Through the winter. Then, in the summer months, when it stays lighter out in the evenings, adjust the time a bit. Do 7:00 PM instead."

"Alright. Okay. I'll come."

"Good! I think it can only help you even more."

"Thank you, Dr. Lee."

"It's my pleasure," said Dr. Lee, smiling.

"I've wasted enough of your time this evening," said Samantha.

"My time is never wasted on you, Sam. I am around whenever you need me."

"Thanks," said Samantha as she stood up, giving her therapist a hug.

"Do you need me to unlock the door for you?" asked Dr. Lee.

"Yes, I do."

"So, what are you going to do when you get home?" asked Dr. Lee as they both walked out of the office and towards the front door of the building.

"Call Aaron."

"Sounds good to me. Remember to be honest with him too. Share what you feel comfortable sharing."

"I will."

They approached the front door together, as Dr. Lee reached into her pants pocket. Pulling out her keys, she unlocked the door for Samantha. As she was walking out to the parking lot, Dr. Lee reminded her about her next appointment.

"Now don't forget our next appointment in a few weeks, Sam."

"Of course. I'll be here."

"You take care of yourself, Samantha. If you need help between now and then, do what you did tonight and stop by. My schedule is always open for you."

"Thank you, Dr. Lee."

Samantha turned and walked out into the parking lot as Dr. Lee shut the door to the clinic, locking it in the process as she was now going to prepare to close her counseling business for the day.

Samantha walked through the parking lot draped in the winter darkness, the only light shining from the parking lot lamps that hung on poles high above the ground. Her breath was visible in the cold winter air as a snowflake landed on her nose. It was the first snowfall of the season. Tiny flakes glided down in the night sky. She looked up and watched as each flake came down around her. Some falling on her face tickled her. She giggled, and for the first time in a long time, she felt a sense of peace and optimism for the future.

She closed her warm winter coat tightly around herself as she continued to walk to her car. When she got to it, she stopped and looked around the empty parking lot. A soft hum of winter weather filled the surrounding atmosphere as she unlocked her car door and sat in the driver's seat. Pausing for a moment, she reached into her jacket pocket and pulled out her cell phone. Turning it on, Samantha looked through her contact list and found Aaron. She called, and the phone rang twice before an excited young man answered the phone.

"Sam?" the man said. "Are you okay?"

"I'll be okay. Can we talk?" asked Samantha.

"Of course we can. What is it? Are you sure you're okay?"

"I'm perfectly fine."

There was a long pause as Samantha took a moment to compose herself before she spoke. Tears poured down her cheeks as she took a deep breath, exhaled, and then braced herself to face her fears and say the hardest thing she had ever had to tell someone in the last eleven years of her life.

"I love you."